KT-440-831

THE MARSHAL'S DAUGHTER

Marshal Jeremiah Hammond's daughter Esther has gone off the rails and participated in a robbery. The puritanical lawman knows it is his duty to bring her to justice — though he soon finds that doing one's duty is more complicated than he first thought. But when Esther commits murder, Hammond finds himself fighting with all his strength to protect his family — and, putting all his principles aside, assisting his precious daughter in evading the law . . .

Books by Harriet Cade
in the Linford Western Library:

THE HOMESTEADER'S DAUGHTER

C463532585

SOUTH LANARKSHIRE
Leisure & Culture
www.library.southlanarkshire.gov.uk

South Lanarkshire Libraries
This book is to be returned on
or before the last date stamped
below or may be renewed by
telephone or online.

Delivering services for South Lanarkshire

1 4 MAR 2016   − 2 SEP 2017   LN−MOBC

29. MAR 19.

2 7 APR 2016   HTH   − 7 NOV 2017   18. SEP 19

EG−CL
REQ   − 3 JAN 2018   RG   CL−LR

− 8 OCT 2016

1 7 MAR 2018

− 8 NOV 2016   2 8 SEP 2019

CL−ST   0 9 MAY 2018   2 7 DEC 2019

2 1 DEC 2016   1 2 JUL 2018   2 8 FEB 2020

W
STLE

POOL STOCK

JT12344/Dec13

SPECIAL MESSAGE TO READERS

THE ULVERSCROFT FOUNDATION
(registered UK charity number 264873)
was established in 1972 to provide funds for
research, diagnosis and treatment of eye diseases.
Examples of major projects funded by
the Ulverscroft Foundation are:-

- The Children's Eye Unit at Moorfields Eye Hospital, London
- The Ulverscroft Children's Eye Unit at Great Ormond Street Hospital for Sick Children
- Funding research into eye diseases and treatment at the Department of Ophthalmology, University of Leicester
- The Ulverscroft Vision Research Group, Institute of Child Health
- Twin operating theatres at the Western Ophthalmic Hospital, London
- The Chair of Ophthalmology at the Royal Australian College of Ophthalmologists

You can help further the work of the Foundation
by making a donation or leaving a legacy.
Every contribution is gratefully received. If you
would like to help support the Foundation or
require further information, please contact:

THE ULVERSCROFT FOUNDATION
The Green, Bradgate Road, Anstey
Leicester LE7 7FU, England
Tel: (0116) 236 4325

website: www.foundation.ulverscroft.com

HARRIET CADE

THE MARSHAL'S DAUGHTER

Complete and Unabridged

LINFORD
Leicester

First published in Great Britain in 2014 by
Robert Hale Limited
London

First Linford Edition
published 2016
by arrangement with
Robert Hale Limited
London

Copyright © 2014 by Harriet Cade
All rights reserved

A catalogue record for this book is available
from the British Library.

ISBN 978–1–4448–2715–6

Published by
F. A. Thorpe (Publishing)
Anstey, Leicestershire

Set by Words & Graphics Ltd.
Anstey, Leicestershire
Printed and bound in Great Britain by
T. J. International Ltd., Padstow, Cornwall

This book is printed on acid-free paper

1

It was late afternoon on a raw, grey day at the back-end of October 1879 and Marshal Jeremiah Hammond was feeling mightily ticked off with the world in general and his own life in particular. For eight days he had been tracking a fugitive across Kansas and now into the Indian Territories. This fellow had robbed a bank and then taken a child hostage at gunpoint in order to effect his escape. A posse had caught up with him, the little girl had been killed in the ensuing gunfight and he had still managed to get away. Now he was hiding out in the territories and it was Hammond's suspicion that he was camped somewhere nearby. The pursuit had been a long and arduous one; he would be glad to catch the man and then either kill him on the spot or take him back to be hanged.

The land hereabouts was pretty bleak: scrub, interspersed with patches of woodland. As the marshal approached one such little bit of forest, a man on horseback rode out of it towards him. He was an Indian, Choctaw by the look of him. As he drew level with Hammond, the marshal said, 'I am looking for a white man who is hiding out around here. Have you seen anybody camping or living rough?'

'I no speak English good,' declared the man and made to move on. Hammond rode his horse into the other man's path and told him, 'Yes, I am on to all those tricks which tend towards a man losing the power of speech when questioned by the law. It won't answer with me; I can tell you that for nothing.' He showed the Indian his badge and said, 'I'm a US marshal and I am in pursuit of a dangerous criminal. I will ask you again, have you seen any white man roughing it round these parts?'

For somebody who had so recently disclaimed the ability to speak good

English, the Choctaw's next sentence was astonishingly fluent, because he said to Marshal Hammond, 'I don't believe that your authority covers this territory. Do you have a warrant?'

'Educated man, hey?' said Hammond, in a tone of voice which suggested that he did not altogether regard education as being a wholly unalloyed good when it led folk to question his authority. He drew the Colt dragoon which was tucked in his belt, cocking it with his thumb as he did so. Then he pointed it at the Indian's face, saying, 'This here is my warrant. Now answer my question.'

'Now you speak of it,' said the man, 'I mind that I saw somebody camping over in the woods there.'

'There now,' said Hammond, 'I thought we might come to it. I am obliged to you for your help.'

He allowed the Choctaw to ride on and then dismounted from his horse and led her along at a walk towards the trees. When he got there, he tied the mare to a branch and crept stealthily into the woods. There was a smell of wood smoke, which suggested to the marshal a campfire or some such. It was a fair guess that whoever undertook to sleep out of doors at this time of year would be wanting to have a cheerful fire going to ward off the chill night air. He made his way towards where he thought the smell of smoke was coming from.

After he had moved a few hundred yards, Hammond could see through the trees the ruddy glow of a fire. Approaching carefully with his pistol cocked and ready in his hand, the marshal noted with satisfaction that there was no sound of any voices, indicating to him a lone person sitting by the fire. So it proved, for as he crept closer he saw that only a raggedy, scarecrow figure sat hunched by the fire. It was at this point that things began to go wrong, because Marshal Hammond stepped upon a dry stick, which cracked asunder with a noise like a pistol shot. The shadowy figure leaped

4

to its feet and cried, 'Who's there? Answer now or you'll be getting a minie ball through your heart!'

Hammond ducked behind a stout oak tree and called, 'US marshal! Throw down your weapon and step forward.'

The instant response was a bullet, which slammed into the tree behind which Marshal Hammond was sheltering. The man shouted,

'US marshal be damned! Come an inch closer and you will be killed.'

Jeremiah Hammond was not a man to hesitate when he knew that right was on his side. He peeped around the tree and saw that the man was now silhouetted against his fire. He had a rifle in his hands and was peering vainly into the darkness. With no further ado, the marshal drew down on the man and shot him. When he did not fall immediately, Hammond fired twice more; once at his chest and then again at his head.

A cursory search of the campsite

soon revealed that the dead man had indeed been the bank robber whom Hammond had been pursuing. A large carpet bag was crammed with bills and gold coins. Many a lawman in this position would have dipped into the bag and taken a few dollars for himself, but Jeremiah Hammond was not of that brand. He would no more have dreamed of taking money in that way than he would have robbing a bank at gunpoint; to him, the two acts were indistinguishable. People might say many harsh things about him, but even his worst enemy would concede that the marshal's honesty was bred in the bone.

Hammond dragged the dead man back to the fire and slung him over the pony which was tethered nearby. Then he stamped out the fire, picked up the carpet bag of cash and led the pony out of the woods to where his own horse was waiting.

On the train back to his home town, Marshal Hammond sat back in his seat and relaxed in that perfect assurance that only the exceedingly self-righteous can ever truly feel; an unshakable conviction that he was an upright, honest and God-fearing man whose actions were always beyond reproach. He lived by the Good Book and as long as his actions were in accordance with Scripture then — as far as Jeremiah Hammond was concerned — there was an end to the matter. The ideas of man were as nothing when compared to the eternal standards by which he lived his own life.

This belief in his own rectitude made the marshal a difficult man to get along with sometimes and it was not only drunkards and thieves who felt uncomfortable in his presence. Even the minister at his church had been known to remark privately that he feared that if the Lord himself returned to earth, there was a strong possibility that He might find that He fell somewhat short when measured by Jeremiah Hammond's own strict code of morality.

As the train pulled into the station, Marshal Hammond felt relieved to be back in his own territory. Everybody knew him in Linton and he was respected both as a lawman and a man of God who lived his faith in public just as he did in his own home, once the doors were closed. Nobody in this town had ever heard any ill of Jeremiah Hammond, of that he was utterly assured.

As he strolled home from the station, the marshal began to fear that something was amiss with his appearance. Folk walking by greeted him well enough, but they seemed to be giving him odd looks and after he had passed, he had the impression that some were whispering about him to each other. He stopped by a storefront and checked his reflection in the window, in case he had a smudge on his face or something of the sort. The sober, black-clad figure looking back at him did not strike him as being any different from usual. Still, as he progressed down the street, the feeling became ever stronger that he was the object of remark. He was glad to reach his house.

Jeremiah Hammond lived with his seventeen-year-old daughter Esther. Her mother had died in childbirth and Hammond's spinster sister Caroline had moved in with him soon after to help raise the child. She was a deal softer on the girl than he could have wished for, but by and large the arrangement had worked out well enough. As he walked through the door, Marshal Hammond removed his hat and called out, 'Caro, Esther, I'm back!'

His sister appeared from the kitchen. She had a look of great anxiety about her and Hammond wondered what was to do. Some trifling matter or other, he guessed. That was spinster women for you, always getting into a fret about something or nothing. 'Well,' he said. 'What's the news? You look worried. Have you broken a plate or blocked up the drains by pouring fat down them?

9

Out with it now, I promise not to be too vexed with you. Where's Esther?'

'Sit down, Jeremiah. A terrible thing has befallen us and I hardly know how to tell you about it.'

A sudden cold fear clutched at the marshal's heart. 'It's Esther, isn't it? What ails her? Has she took sick?'

'No, it has no reference to her health. For aught that I know she is as robust as ever.'

'For aught that you know? Why, what's the case? Where is the child?'

'She is gone. Please sit down, Jeremiah. I need to tell you what has chanced. If you do not sit, then you may be struck all of a heap by the time I have finished.'

Reluctantly, Marshal Hammond sat and waited with immense foreboding to hear what his sister had to say. She too sat down, facing him.

'I had best give it to you at once,' said Caroline Hammond. 'Esther has run off with a real bad lot, that young fellow who was working over by the depot.

Chris Turner is his name.'

'Turner?' asked the marshal in amazement. 'Not that mean-looking boy that I had to take up for being in liquor one Sunday afternoon?'

'That's the one,' said his sister grimly. 'Well, to tell you the whole of the business, the two of them robbed the office down at the depot. The night watchman there was struck on the head, but he will live. They made off with over a hundred dollars and have now lit out for the Lord knows where.'

Hammond shook his head slowly in utter disbelief. 'But Caroline, there must be some mistake. It could never have been Esther. You must have it wrong. Not my daughter. Why, she teaches in Sunday school. She has never even gone out walking with a boy, never mind running off! No, you have got this all mixed up.'

His sister looked a little irritable, despite her own grief at the loss of her beloved niece. 'There's no mistake, Jeremiah. Leastways, if there is, it is all

11

on your part. That child has done a sight more than go walking with boys as well. I am sorrowed at how she has turned out, but I would be a liar were I to say that I am surprised.'

Marshal Hammond stood up suddenly. 'I don't know what is the matter with you, Caro. To talk so of your own flesh and blood. I won't hear any more. It is as I say, there has been a mistake. I am going down to the office to straighten things out. Do not let me hear you speak of my daughter in this way again. We will forget what was said.' With which, he left the house at a brisk walk and went downtown to his office.

As he headed along, Hammond turned over in his mind what his sister had said. It was just not possible and he was sure that there had been some error, somewhere down the road. His daughter! It was unthinkable. He had raised the child according to Scripture, ever mindful of Proverbs, Chapter twenty two, verse six. 'Train up a child in the way he should go and he will not depart from it, even in old age'. There had been little enough frivolity in his daughter's childhood and he took satisfaction in the realization that while the daughters of his friends often seemed to be straying from the path of righteousness, the same could not be said of Esther. She was as God-fearing a Christian girl as you could hope to meet. No, something was wrong here and he meant to clear the matter up as soon as might be. Just see what happened once he was away from town for a week or so! Everything became tangled up.

The instant that he crossed the threshold and entered the office, Hammond knew that he had been deceiving himself and that what his sister had told him was true, at least in part. His two deputies looked up when he came in and he saw in their faces that most loathsome of emotions in his eyes: pity for him. It was, unless he missed his guess, mixed also with a certain amount of satisfaction at seeing a Godly man brought low. Well, that was the way of the world. He could withstand this trial as he had done many others in the past.

The marshal greeted the two younger men by saying cheerfully, 'Well, what's to do, boys?'

'Jeremiah,' said Greg Barnes. 'I am guessing that you will have heard something about what has happened while you were away . . .'

'Something, yes,' said Hammond. 'Suppose you give me the official version?'

The two men exchanged glances and stirred uneasily. 'Well,' said the other deputy. 'There are so to speak two official versions and we wanted to set them both before you so that you might give your stamp of approval to one of them, as it were.'

'Two versions?' said Hammond. 'Something does not listen right here. Suppose you two just tell me what has happened as best you can. We will worry later about these two versions.'

'All right,' said Greg Barnes. 'It is like this. On Monday night, the office down at the depot was broken into and a hundred and ten dollars stolen. The night watchman turned up and says that there were two people present. One was Chris Turner and the other your Esther. Turner lamped him with a piece of lead pipe and knocked him senseless. When he came to, it was nearly dawn.'

'Is he certain-sure about this?' said Hammond, 'Meaning that is about the identity of those who attacked him?'

'He will take oath that it was Turner who hit him and also that Esther was there with him,' said Barnes flatly.

'Where are they now?' asked the marshal.

'There was a train heading west stopped for half an hour on Monday night to take on water. We are thinking that Turner and your daughter climbed on it. Leastways, they have neither of them been seen since.'

Marshal Hammond sat for a full minute without speaking. Neither of his deputies felt inclined to say anything during this time. At last, he said, 'And what are these two versions of events of which you made mention?'

Barnes continued. 'The night watchman had been drinking on duty. I told him that if he said anything about your daughter being there, then I would see that he lost his job. Mind, the story is all over town now, but we can at least avoid having Esther down on the official statements. It will be enough if Turner answers for the robbery.'

'Why would you do that?' asked Hammond.

'Because we would not like to see your daughter in trouble. We thought that we could extricate her and that after a spell, things would die down and folk would forget that she had been named. Either that or we could have her down as a witness or something.'

'Is that how little you two know me?' said the marshal sternly, 'You think that I will dodge like a fox and give corrupt testimony to favour my own family? It is not to be thought of.' He stood up. 'Hand me the file on this case, I am going down to the court with it.'

'What for, Jeremiah? We can handle this.'

'It seems not. I am going to have warrants sworn out for the pair of them and then I am going to bring them in myself. When I get back, we had best have a talk about perjury and tampering with witnesses. I can see that things have gotten right slack in my absence. Two official versions indeed!'

Marshal Jeremiah Hammond picked up the papers and left the office without bidding either of his deputies farewell. Once he had left, Greg Barnes shook his head in disbelief and said, 'There goes the hardest man that ever drew breath in this world. Swearing out a warrant for his own child! In all my born days, I never heard the like.'

2

Once he had finished at the courthouse and sworn out the warrants charging Christopher James Turner and Esther Maria Hammond with robbery with violence, the marshal returned to his house. He was minded to make his peace with Caroline and show her that he held no grudge about the unfortunate developments in his family life.

'I do not blame you for this,' Hammond told his sister. 'I will observe that you might perhaps have been a mite stricter with the child and that there were occasions when you undermined my authority, but on the whole . . .'

Caroline Hammond was the mildest of women and always mindful of the debt she owed to her brother for taking her in and sheltering her in his house, but even she could not forebear to interrupt at this point. 'You think that

18

Esther has taken this road because we were too soft with her? Is that what you think, Jeremiah? That had there been even more strictness and forbidding of pleasure and light-heartedness and I don't know what-all else, then she might not have cut loose in this way?'

Hammond looked at his sister in astonishment. In all the years she had shared his home, never once had she spoken so to him. He said, 'Why Caroline, I do not know what is wrong with you today. Yes, certainly I think that we were too easy on the child and that this wickedness is a consequence of our neglecting to correct her more firmly. You must admit that you have often urged me to let her get away with faults that you dismissed as trifling. You share the blame for this, but the main responsibility is mine. I should have been firmer. This evil is a result of my own weakness.'

'God save us!' cried Caroline Hammond and rushed upstairs in a flood of tears.

Marshal Hammond took a sombre leave-taking of his sister when he set out for the railroad station an hour later. To his disgust, Caroline made the same infamous suggestion to him that his deputies had hinted at: that he should bring in Chris Turner and somehow contrive to leave his own daughter out of the reckoning. 'I am afeared that there is a deal more wickedness in the world than ever I suspected,' declared Hammond in a shocked voice, when his sister had the effrontery to put the plan to him. 'I tell you now, Caroline, that I am grieved to the very heart. First my own men and now my sister — all urging me to perjure myself and put my very soul in jeopardy. I tell you plainly, it is not to be thought of. I will behave righteously although all the world stands against me.'

Marshal Hammond had figured that the two fugitives would not be wanting to travel too far and were likely to stop at the nearest big town, hoping to lose themselves there. The railroad line went past a few piddling little way-halts before reaching Delano and Wichita. If his instincts did not play him false, this would be where Esther and that wretched boy would be found. The marshal accordingly booked a ticket from Linton to Wichita, catching the train at three that afternoon.

It was about a hundred and thirty miles from Linton to Wichita and so Marshal Hammond looked forward to a couple of hours of relaxation — which in his case usually consisted of studying the Old Testament. He always found a lot more to agree with in that part of the Bible, as opposed to the wishy washy teachings of the Gospels. The marshal settled down in his seat and reminded himself what Scripture had to say about disobedient and rebellious children. He was immersed in the very sensible rules set out in Leviticus on this subject, when he gradually became aware of a disturbance further down the carriage. With the greatest reluctance, he closed his Bible and went to investigate.

It might be mentioned at this point that when, as was currently the case, Jeremiah Hammond was not sporting his star, folk oft-times took him to be a preacher rather than a lawman. This was a natural consequence of his black clothes, sober mien and the generally respectable and God-fearing air which he had. The resemblance to a man of the cloth was greatly increased on this particular occasion by the fact that as he moved down the carriage, he was still clutching the Bible in his hand. He did not like wearing his pistol on trains either and so his appearance was entirely that of a peaceable and devout middle-aged man. This was certainly the impression which the four rowdy young cowboys who were making a nuisance of themselves gained when Hammond approached them, saying quietly, 'You boys might want to moderate your language a little. There are women and children nearby who do not want to hear your cursing and blaspheming.'

Two women sitting near to the cowboys gave the marshal a grateful look. As for the boys themselves, they did not know what to make of the play. One of them said in a jocular fashion, 'Looky here now you fellows, stop all that bad language. Elsewise this parson will be reading you a sermon.' He turned to Hammond and said, 'Ain't that right, reverend? You will preach to us all if we do not calm down and behave nicely?'

Jeremiah Hammond regarded the young man benignly and said, 'No son, I am not a parson and you will get no sermon from me.'

'Well that's a mercy,' said one of the other men and made a loud, farting noise, which reduced his companions to helpless laughter.

One of them then said, 'Well, if you ain't about to reprove us for our sinful ways, then I guess it is all right for me to carry on using words like . . . ' He spoke out loud a word so vile that Marshal Hammond could scarcely believe what he heard. One of the women nearby gasped in horror and covered her little girl's ears.

Hammond placed his Bible down gently on a nearby seat and then turned to the four young men. He shot out his left hand and gripped the throat of the one who had said the offensive word. The boy scrabbled at the marshal's fingers, thinking to pluck his hand away, only to find that the muscles of the hand around his throat were as rigid and immoveable as iron rods. He began to choke and gasp for air. The fellow next to him began to stand up, until Jeremiah's right fist went forward like the piston of a steam engine, felling him with a mighty blow to his face.

Hammond released his grip upon the first of the young men to provoke his wrath, leaving him purple-faced and gulping for air. Then the marshal looked at the other two boys, who had not yet had a chance to react to the unexpected turn of events. 'Either of you two fellows have anything to say?' he enquired mildly. They did not. He picked up his Bible and then said to the woman who had been offended by the language being used, 'If you have any further cause to feel uneasy, I shall be sitting over yonder. Just let me know and I shall be glad to come back and deal with matters.' Then he returned to his seat and opened the Good Book at Deuteronomy.

* * *

While her father was straightening out the young men on the railroad train, Esther Hammond was laying on the bed in a seedy boarding house down by the waterfront in Delano. She was restless and bored. 'I hope that we are going out tonight,' she told the young man who lay next to her on the bed.

'We cannot go out to the saloon every night, you know,' said Chris Turner. 'That money will not last forever.'

'Well I guess we can get some more in the same way,' the girl told him impatiently. 'I did not leave my home just to sit around in a dreary room like this.'

'What do you reckon your father will do when he gets back?' asked the boy curiously.

'He probably won't even notice that I have left. He never sets much mind to me, beyond saying 'mind your manners' and 'have you said your prayers tonight?''

'He is a powerful strong one for religion, ain't he?'

'Lord, yes. It is all he ever thinks on.'

'I wonder,' said Turner, 'that he did not become a minister rather than a lawman.'

The girl laughed. 'He nearly did. Only thing was, he said that the Lord could make more use of him as a marshal than he could if he was tending to a church.'

'You don't think much to him, do you?'

'I hate him!' said Esther Hammond passionately.

The boy looked faintly shocked. 'That's not right. My own Ma and Pa are aggravating, but I would not say I hated them.'

Esther looked at the boy lying next to her on the bed. 'Listen,' she said, 'Did you have birthdays when you were little?'

Chris Turner's face lit up with remembrance of a simple pleasure. 'Why yes, of course I did. There was not much money for presents or such, but still and all, my folks made the day special.'

'I did not have a single birthday.'

'Not have a birthday? Why, whatever can you mean?'

'My Pa, he said that celebrating birthdays was heathenish. We did not mark them at all. My aunt tried once, but he put a stop to it. Talked about the vanities of the world.'

'You had Christmas though, didn't you?'

'Yes,' said Esther. 'We had Christmas. No gifts there either, because the day belonged to the Lord. It would have been sinful to cheapen it by giving worldly things to each other. Christmas Day meant three visits to church and more Bible reading than usual. I used to dread it.'

Chris Turner did not know what to reply to all this. At last he said, 'Do you think though that your father will look for you? Meaning that he will try and take you home if he finds where you are?'

'I would rather die,' said the girl shortly.

★ ★ ★

As the train approached Wichita, Marshal Hammond opened his travelling bag and took out the gunbelt that it contained. He buckled it on and then pinned the star to his jacket. Now that the journey was over, he was on official business and wished nobody to make any mistake about his authority. He read through the warrants again to make sure that they were both in order. Then, once the train had fully stopped, he stood up, walked to the end of the carriage and stepped down onto the platform.

Wichita and nearby Delano were cattle towns at the end of the Chisholm Trail. They had grown in recent years until they now formed one sprawling settlement which straddled the Arkansas River. The whole area had a reputation for lawlessness and disorder, particularly when the cattle drives arrived at the railheads. A few years before Jeremiah Hammond stepped off the train there, one Wyatt Earp had been the town marshal and even he had found the place hard to control. In addition to the permanent population, there were a huge and constantly fluctuating number of cowboys and drifters in the twin towns. It was the ideal place to come if you wished to lose yourself, which is perhaps why

Chris Turner and Esther Hammond had headed there after robbing the depot in Linton.

Marshal Hammond had no authority to enforce the law in either Wichita or Delano — for that there were town marshals. He did have the right though to search for fugitives and if found, then to arrest them and take them back for trial. The authorities in the two towns were obliged by law to offer him assistance in these endeavours, should he ask for it. Not that Hammond expected to be doing so. If he could not track down and take into custody two youngsters who were little more than children, well then it would be time for him to resign and look for another line of work altogether!

The Wichita and Delano marshal's office was only a short walk from the railroad station. The two towns shared many services and the rumour was that they would soon be officially united or, as the citizens of Delano feared, their town would in effect be annexed by its larger and more populous neighbour. There were two men in the office when Hammond walked in and so friendly were they with each other that he naturally, although wrongly, assumed both to be lawmen. He introduced himself and produced the warrants. One of the two men looked them over carefully, before glancing up in surprise. 'We have met before, Marshal Hammond, although you might not remember me. I see that this warrant is for somebody called Hammond. Not a relative or something, I hope?'

'It is my daughter,' said Jeremiah Hammond in a stony voice.

'Your daughter?' exclaimed the other. 'That's blazing strange. I don't know that I ever heard of such a thing before. Could you not have sent one of your deputies? It would sit ill with me to have to arrest my own flesh and blood.'

'Well I am a man who knows his duty,' said Marshal Hammond, 'and I do not shrink from it, however hard it might be.'

The other man who had been in the office when he entered now joined in the conversation. 'You say that you are in town to arrest your own daughter, sir? That is a most unusual circumstance.'

'All right, Jed,' growled the deputy marshal who had been speaking with Hammond. 'That will do. Perhaps I should introduce Mr Jed Culpepper of the Wichita Beacon. Jed is our local newspaper man. Not that he has any business interrupting our conversation, mind.'

Hammond turned to the reporter and said, 'I will not be best pleased if I read in your newspaper about my arrival here. If you do anything to compromise my work, you will answer to me for it.'

'Surely, sir, surely,' said Culpepper smoothly. 'Nothing would be further from my mind than to jeopardize an official investigation. Perhaps our paper can help you by publishing a description of those whom you are seeking.

The Wichita and Delano Beacon, incorporating the Kansas Intelligencer, has no fewer than twenty five thousand registered readers.'

Marshal Hammond turned a cold eye upon the talkative man. 'I do not care how many people buy your newspaper,' he said. 'Let one word about my presence be advertised there and I will come looking for you.'

After having delivered himself of this warning, Hammond bade both men good evening and went to arrange a room at an hotel. After he had gone, Jed Culpepper said to his old friend, 'Really though, Pete, did you ever hear of a man chasing his own daughter for to arrest her? It's as good as a novel!'

'You plainly never heard before of Jeremiah Hammond,' said the deputy, 'He is famous for being a man who will do what is right in his own eyes, come what may. I would not advise you to get crosswise to him, Jed, and that is all that I will say on the subject.'

★ ★ ★

Although he did not have to pay for his
own travel and accommodation when
on official business, it was part of
Marshal Hammond's rigid honesty that
he always made sure that he spent as
little as possible of the money entrusted
to him. It went without saying that he
would not walk somewhere and then
charge for a carriage, but neither would
he be profligate with his choice of hotel.
His duty was to save society money, not
squander it away on luxury. With this in
mind, he wandered around downtown
Wichita, seeking a cheap boarding
house.

Eventually, in a narrow, gloomy side
street, Hammond came across a dingy
looking clapboard house with a faded
sign outside announcing that rooms
were to be let within. He rapped
smartly on the door, congratulating
himself on having found a place which
would most likely cost half of what he
would have paid in a more central and

bustling part of the town. As soon as the door was opened though, he began to fear that he had made a dreadful mistake.

Sweet smelling smoke trickled out into the night as the door of the boarding house was opened and a wizened little Chinaman peered out. 'Come in, come in,' said the man. 'Very cheap rooms, all clean, no cockroaches.'

For a moment, Hammond thought of bolting and looking for another place, but his ingrained respect for old age prevented him and he stepped into the hallway of the house, wrinkling his nose at the smoke. A horrible thought struck him and he said, 'What's with all this smoke? This is not an opium den or some such, I hope?'

The old Chinaman cackled with amusement. 'No opium here, no. This is incense. I burn it to honour the Master.'

'Master?' asked Hammond, 'What Master? I am looking for a room for a few nights; do you have one to rent?'

'Yes, yes. Plenty of rooms. Nobody comes now, whole house empty. Come through please.' The man led him into a back parlour. The marshal noted that the old man had his hair tied back in a pigtail and was wearing a skull cap. He looked just what you would expect a Chinaman in a story book to look like.

In an alcove at the back of the room stood a little statue, no more than a foot high, of a traditionally dressed Chinaman. At his feet was set a bowl of chrysanthemums and next to them was a small metal plate which looked to have a few glowing coals upon it. 'See here,' said the Chinaman, 'Smoke comes from here, burn to honour the Master. No opium!' He gave a little giggle.

'So this here is your 'Master'?' said Hammond, 'Who is it, some heathen god?'

'No god,' said the little man, sounding shocked, 'Great man. Kung Fu Tse. You call him Confucius.'

'I seem to recollect hearing of him.'

36

'This is not business. You want room, I have room. I am Mr Chang. Come this way please, sir.'

*　*　*

Despite his protestations about their running out of money, it did not really take a great deal of coaxing on Esther Hammond's part to persuade Chris to take her to a saloon that night. He was no keener than her to remain cooped up in the little room they were renting.

Some saloons did not encourage women, but others, like The Lucky Strike, positively welcomed them with open arms. There was drinking, dancing and card play on offer and to Esther it was the most brilliantly exciting place that she had ever seen in her life. Everything about it shouted a full-blooded rejection of the values in which she had been raised. There was gambling, there were women dancing, some of whom she was sure had painted their faces and one or two of whom were even smoking cigarettes. And of course, there was the drinking.

Esther had never touched a drop of intoxicating liquor in the whole course of her life until she had started around six months previously. She had at first found the taste revolting, but the effects were little short of magical. It acted on her like some enchanted potion that gave her the confidence and strength that she lacked in real life. She had never realized that anything could make her feel so good. Since they had arrived in Delano, she had been drinking every day.

In addition to the liquor, there was the card play at the faro table.

'Do you know,' said the girl to Chris Turner, 'until Tuesday night, I had only caught one glimpse of a deck of playing cards in my life? Can you believe that?'

'Knowing, as I do, your father, yes, I can believe it.'

'He wouldn't have a pack of cards in the house, so I never saw any as a child. One day we went visiting somebody sick from the church. Pa used to get me to go with him on those visits, but I hated seeing sick people. This time we went to an old woman's house. She was dying and my father thought that it would be wholesome for me to witness how a true Christian met her death. Old Mrs Bridges was playing solitaire when we arrived and my father's eyes nearly popped out of his head. We didn't stay long and after we left, he told me that those things she was handling were 'the Devil's picture book'.'

'Hush up, now Esther,' said Turner, 'I am trying to follow the play here.'

The two young people were standing on the fringe of a group surrounding the faro table. All the cards were marked out on a large table and it was possible to bet on what card you thought would be drawn from the wooden box which they called the shoe. The dealer took two cards at a time. One was a winner and those who had bet on it received back double their stake and the other was a loser, which meant that those who had placed their money on that one lost it.

The trick of faro is to work out which cards have already been drawn, so that you can calculate the odds on the remaining cards being drawn. Chris Turner was trying to do this, but after she had had a couple of drinks, the girl at his side just could not stop talking and this was a distraction.

'Don't you think that those young men on the picture cards look awful handsome?' asked Esther.

'Young men? Oh, you mean the knaves.'

'Knaves?' Esther Hammond laughed. 'Is that what they call them? What about those older men with beards, how are they called?'

'They are the kings. Keep your voice down, Esther. Folk are staring at us.'

'I don't mind,' declared the tipsy girl, 'Let them stare. I am surely worth looking at or wouldn't you say so?'

Chris Turner sighed. Picking up with

the marshal's daughter had seemed a fine joke at the time, but the whole thing was now wearing decidedly thin. He had lost his home, was on the run and stuck with a girl who, for all her religious upbringing, struck Turner as being more full of devilment and sheer mischief than any young woman he had ever met in his life. As he tried to ignore Esther's chatter and concentrate on the cards, Chris Turner could not help but feel that he might have taken a wrong turn somewhere over the last week or so.

3

The fact was, Marshal Hammond had no very clear idea of how he was to track down his daughter and the boy who had, as he saw the case, led her astray. After leaving his things in the room which he had agreed to pay for on a daily basis, Hammond thought that he could do worse than roam around the town a little and see what was what. He had not been to Wichita for some years and the place had changed greatly from his recollections of it and not for the better, either.

To Jeremiah Hammond's eye, long practised in the detection of wickedness and sin, the busy streets of the town had the appearance of a regular Sodom or Gommorah. At every street corner there were taverns and the sidewalks were crowded with women who behaved in lewd and unbecoming ways. It was an object lesson in what a town could descend to if there were not strong men in charge who set a watch upon Sabbath breaking and the intemperate consumption of ardent spirits. Thank the good Lord that Linton was not like this.

So depressing did the marshal find Wichita that he resolved to have an early night and begin his search in earnest the following day. Having decided this, he headed back to the boarding house where he was staying.

The old Chinaman opened the door for Hammond and then, to the marshal's surprise, invited him to share a pot of tea. This promised to be such a novelty, that he found himself agreeing.

When they were settled in the back room, under the scrutiny of the statue of Confucius, Mr Chang said, 'What brings you to our town, sir? I see that you are a policeman.'

For some reason, Hammond found himself telling Chang about his quest to find his daughter and return her to face justice in Linton. The old man said nothing, but after hearing the tale, stood up and fetched a book from a little bookcase on the other side of the room. He said, 'Analects of Kung Fu Tse. Very like your Jesus. Said much the same things.'

Jeremiah Hammond was not about to allow this heathen to compare the Lord's teaching with that of some Chinaman from the ancient past and so he said, 'I'm sure that is not so. Our Lord's teaching was all new, you know. Nobody had ever thought like him before.'

Mr Chang seemed amused at this and said, 'Sum up your lord's teaching for me.'

'Well, I guess that what it came down to was: do unto others as you would be done by. Yes, I think that pretty well sums up the case.'

The Chinaman nodded his head in a pleased way. 'Yes, yes. Same that Kung Fu Tse said, only five hundred years before your lord. He said, 'Do not do to others what would anger you if it were done to you'. Same thing, I think. Only many years before your lord.'

In the normal way of things, Hammond found talk of this kind irritating and a little disrespectful to the Lord, but there was something about the old man which invited trust. He said to him, 'Well Mr Chang, you might have a point there and no mistake. I will allow that there is some similarity. But I'll warrant your Confucius had nothing to say about the present case — that is to say of me hunting after my daughter for the sake of righteousness. My Bible sets the matter out for me clearly, but how would your 'Master' have tackled the problem?'

The old man gave him a very strange look. Then he said, 'Why sir, Kung Fu Tse was asked this very thing. He gave a good answer to it as well. Would you like to hear what he said?'

It was on the tip of Jeremiah Hammond's tongue to say, 'No, I don't care what some dirty foreigner said about the business', but he felt that this would be discourteous and also maybe a little cowardly. He had, after all, asked the question. He said gruffly, 'Well, well. What did your 'Master' say then?'

Mr Chang turned the pages of his book until he located the right passage. Then he read it out. 'The Governor of Sheh said to the Master, 'In our village we have an example of a straight person. When the father stole a sheep, the son gave evidence against him'. Kung Fu Tse answered, saying, 'In our village, those who are straight are quite different. Fathers cover up for their sons and sons cover up for their fathers. In such behaviour, straightness is to be found as matter of course'.'

★　★　★

As the evening wore on, Esther Hammond became increasingly wild, until Turner hardly knew what to do with her. Worst of all was where she insisted on 'helping' him to place bets at the faro table. She had not the least idea of odds or counting the cards and wanted to put money only on particular cards of which she liked the look or felt were somehow lucky. She kept up a constant commentary which drove any other thoughts from Chris Turner's head and made it impossible for him to think what he was about.

'I love this whiskey,' said Esther. 'Do you like whiskey? The Bible says that, 'Wine is a mocker and strong drink is raging', but I do not find it so. Mind, I am inclined to agree with that passage in Scripture which holds that it 'Biteth like a serpent and stingeth like an adder', but I do not think that a bad thing. Chris, Chris, bet on that card, that red one with the beautiful lady.'

'Esther, both the Queen of Hearts and the Queen of Diamonds have already come and gone. It would be throwing money in the gutter. For God's sake hush a little and let me think what I am doing.'

'Who do you think you are, telling me to hush? You think that you are my father? You damned well hush!'

At this point, one of the men at the saloon who were employed to watch out for trouble came over and spoke quietly to Chris. When he had gone, Esther said, 'What did he want?'

'He said that if you do not watch your language and quieten down, then they will throw us both out into the street. Now let me think about the next bet, because we are down to ten dollars.'

Esther was shocked to hear that all their money seemed to have evaporated so rapidly. The time had simply flown by and she was unaware of the fact that she had actually spent over three hours in the saloon. The miracle of it was that they still had a cent left after all that time. Even now, the girl could not remain silent for more than a few seconds. Chris Turner became flustered, put down two five dollar bets and promptly lost them both. The pair now had not a penny to their names.

Neither Esther nor Chris were in the best of moods after leaving the Lucky Strike. They bickered about who was to blame as they walked back to their room, vainly trying to apportion the blame for the loss of their money, as though this would somehow ameliorate their situation. It was the girl who came up with the idea of carrying out another robbery. After all, the last one had been easy and successful enough.

'I don't know, Esther,' said Chris Turner. 'I would like to think this over for a spell.'

'What's to think over, you noodle? We have not the wherewithal to pay for our breakfast tomorrow, something must be done.'

'Knocking over the office at the depot was one thing. I used to work there; I knew where the cash was. How the hell am I supposed to find a place like that here in a town that we don't know?'

'Why does it have to be an office with

a cashbox? What about finding some-body carrying a lot of money? If it's a drunk man, then you will only need push him over and then take his wallet. Don't be such a girl!'

To be fair to Esther Hammond, she would not have talked in this way had she not been drinking heavily, some-thing to which she was unused. Having broken free of her gloomy and forbid-ding home, she did not aim to be forced back there for want of a few dollars cash money.

'I don't know,' said Turner doubt-fully.

As ill luck would have it, at just that very moment one of those who had also been playing at the faro table walked past the couple. To say that the fellow 'walked' past is perhaps exaggerating the case to a degree. It would be more accurate to say that he weaved and staggered by, apparently just about able to remain on his feet. Esther nudged her companion. 'Look there, he is just the one.'

There seemed to be something in what she said, thought Turner, as he watched the drunk threading an uncertain and erratic path across the road. He was heading towards a darkened alleyway, probably, thought the boy, with the intention of making water there. He made a sudden decision. 'Stay here,' he hissed at the girl, running after the fellow.

Now if Esther Hammond had not been pretty well liquored up that night, then things might perhaps have taken a very different course. But there it was, she had been drinking steadily for hours and was not likely to do as she was bid by a boy her own age. She followed Chris Turner into the alleyway, just in time to see him give the drunk man a shove and make a grab into his pocket.

It was shadowy and dark in the space between the buildings and so all that Esther really saw was the struggle between the two men. She and Turner had picked altogether the wrong mark for this sort of game, because the man they were attempting to rob was a soldier on leave and although drunk as a fiddler's bitch, he was still more than a match for the half-hearted efforts of a seventeen year-old boy to rob him.

From what Esther could see, the tables had been turned and now the man had caught Chris in a bear hug and was shouting, 'Thief!' at the top of his voice. Lamps were being lit in a room overlooking the alley and if they were not careful then she and Chris would both be caught and sent back to Linton — a thing she was prepared to take any steps to avoid. So it was that Esther Hammond looked round for a weapon and found leaning against a wall, a broken broom handle. Although she could not have known it in the darkness, the wooden rod had split almost lengthways, leaving a sharp point about the size and shape of a knife at the other end from that which she was holding.

Esther was not really scared,

although she was definitely determined not to go back home. The last week or so had been one long exhilarating adventure and her purpose was just to continue in this way for as long as she could. Anything, rather than the deadly dull and sanctimonious life in which she had been raised. So when she snatched up that broom handle, her only intention was to help her friend escape from the pickle into which he landed. She gripped the broom handle firmly, moved forward a few paces and then jabbed it hard into the back of the man who was holding Chris and hollering blue murder. As she shoved it forward, a window was thrown up above them and a women leaned out with a lamp in her hand. She called out, 'Hey, what's going on down there? There are folk here who wish to sleep, you know.'

Thinking over the incident later, the thing that stuck in Esther's mind was how easily that broom handle went forward. She had braced herself, expecting it to bang into the fellow's back as she pushed it at him, but there had been no resistance at all. Although she did not find this out until later, the reason was that the sharp end had slid right through the man's kidneys and then on into his bowels. It had been as effective as a knife.

As soon as the man let go of him, Turner pushed him to one side and made to leave him lying there. Esther said, 'Get his wallet, Chris.' He reached again into the man's pocket and plucked out the heavy billfold that he found there. Then he and Esther ran into the street, leaving the woman with the lamp to grumble about the behaviour of drunks in the neighbourhood and then go back to bed.

★   ★   ★

After speaking to the owner of the boarding house before going to bed, Jeremiah Hammond felt vaguely unsettled. It was not his custom to

54

discuss religion with non-believers, but something about the old Chinaman had made him trust the man. He wished now that he had not, because he had been disturbed by that story about his Confucius. Whenever his faith was in need of restoration, Hammond found that a few passages of Scripture generally acted as a tonic and so he sat on the bed and opened his Bible at the part of Deuteronomy he had been reading on the train to Wichita. 'If any man has a stubborn and rebellious son who will not obey his mother and father, then they shall take him to the elders of the city.' He read on, 'Then all the men of the city shall stone him to death.'

It was these verses that had told the marshal that he was on the right track when he had sworn out that warrant for Esther. This is just precisely what the Lord would have him do. He flicked on a few pages and then came to another verse which he studied carefully. 'I the LORD your God am a jealous God, visiting the iniquity of the fathers upon the children.'

Suddenly, Hammond felt as though he could not breathe. Surely this could not be right, to punish children for what their fathers had done? He went over to the window and opened it. The cool night air revived him somewhat, but he was still a little giddy and faint. In the whole course of his life, this was the first time that he had read the Good Book and not known straight away that it was the word of God. Was it really right to execute a boy for being stubborn and rebellious? Where was the justice in punishing children for the sins of their fathers? Standing there at the window, Jeremiah Hammond felt as though the earth itself were no longer solid and dependable. If he could not lean upon the word of God, then what hope was there for him? His entire life had been founded upon the teachings of this book and now, due only to a chance conversation with some foreign heathen, he had been stricken with doubt. Well, it would not do. He knew that the Devil lay in wait with this very end in mind. It would take more than this to divert Marshal Jeremiah Hammond from the path of righteousness; that was for sure.

★ ★ ★

When they got back to the little room they were staying in, Esther and Chris lit the lamp and just sat there for a space, out of breath and horrified at the turn of events. It was Esther who broke the silence, saying, 'Well, at least you got his wallet in the end. Let us see how much there is in it.'

Turner felt shaky and sick. He had felt sure that he was going to be caught by the police when that fellow began shouting like that. It was strange how he had just relaxed his grip and Turner had been able to push him to the ground. Even now, he had not worked out what had happened. He reached into his jacket and took out the fat billfold. Then he dropped it in disgust.

'What ails you?' said Esther. 'You are a regular butterfingers. Here let me look.'

'No!' Turner almost shouted. 'Don't you see? Look closely at it.'

The girl picked up the wallet and found that it was sticky. She held it to the lamp and realised that the leather was slippery with blood. Perhaps she was less squeamish than Turner, because she just remarked, 'That is strange. I wonder how come there is blood. Are you hurt or something?'

'It's not my blood. Don't you see, it is his. What the hell happened back there, Esther?'

'Nothing happened. I picked up a stick or something and pushed him with it. Then he let go of you. It is nothing to do with us. He must have injured himself earlier. Listen, we must make sure that none of the blood gets on the bills or we will not be able to use them.'

Chris Turner was staring at the

blood and then lurched over to the washstand, where he was violently and abundantly sick in the china basin. 'I wish, I wish . . . ' he said over and over again.

'What do you wish, you baby?' said Esther.

'I wish I'd never picked up with you, Esther Hammond, that's what I wish. There is something not right about you. You are colder than anybody I ever met before in my life and I wish I was back home with my folks, not stuck here with you.'

Esther was hardly listening to the boy's complaints. She was sorting through the contents of the wallet with growing excitement. 'Chris, there is nearly eight hundred dollars here. This should keep us going for some while, I reckon.'

'Eight hundred? You must have counted it wrong. Let me see.'

But Esther Hammond was right. The wallet was crammed with money and as long as they exercised a little caution, they would not need to worry about running out of funds for at least a month or two. So great was the relief of this, that Turner forgot to be vexed with the girl and they put out the lamp and climbed into bed together.

★ ★ ★

It was Jeremiah Hammond's invariable custom to pray before sleeping, but tonight he found that the words simply would not come. All he could think of was not the words of Scripture, but the look on the faces of people when they heard that he was pursuing his own daughter with a view to bringing her to justice. His deputies, his own sister, the man in the marshal's office here in Wichita and that newspaper man; all had stared at him as though he was some rare freak of nature. Mr Chang had been more polite about it, but it was clear that even he was appalled at the idea of a man bringing in his own child like this.

It was while he was thinking this over that it gradually dawned on the marshal that his motives for being so ruthless about the matter were not just about his love of justice and determination to do his duty. He had been shamed by the look in his deputies' eyes. Esther had shamed him and he wanted her to pay for that, rather than the robbery or assault on some night watchman. He was not following some duty at all; he was seeking revenge upon his child for making others feel superior to him. With this disconcerting realization, Hammond turned out the lamp and got into bed, neglecting for the first time in his adult life to pray to the Lord before sleeping.

4

For the next three days Marshal Hammond tried hard to find his daughter. He learned that Delano was cheaper and less salubrious than Wichita and concentrated his searches there, but to no avail. The frustrating thing was that he did not even know if Esther was in this area. For all he knew to the contrary, she and Chris Turner might have stayed on the train and travelled on to Dodge City or even Albuquerque. It was just a feeling that he had, that she was somewhere nearby.

During this time, Hammond fell into the habit of talking quite a bit to Mr Chang about religion. The old man seemed to have a store of wisdom and also to be one of the most broadminded and compassionate men that he had ever met. True, he was not saved immortally, but even so, the marshal felt an odd affinity for the strange Chinaman.

In the usual way of things, any conversations on the topic of religious belief between Jeremiah Hammond and anybody else consisted almost entirely of Hammond pointing out through many scriptural texts that those opposing his views were damned to eternal hellfire. With Chang though, he knew that this would not only have been the height of rudeness, but — what was even more perplexing — would almost certainly have been untrue. He knew deep within that the old Chinaman was not heading for damnation, whether or no he accepted the Lord Jesus as his saviour.

Actually, Marshal Hammond passed very close to his daughter on more than one occasion during his restless prowling through the streets of Delano. It was a wonder really that they did not bump into each other at some point. She and Turner were still going out to saloons in the evenings and after getting back late, they took to staying in bed until long after midday. Since the marshal was doing a lot of his walking about the streets in the morning, this might go a certain way towards explaining how come their paths did not cross over those days.

On Friday *The Wichita and Delano Beacon, incorporating the Kansas Intelligencer* hit the streets. There were two articles in that edition of the newspaper which were of particular interest to three people in the town. The first piece was a light-hearted, human interest story by Jed Culpepper. It was Culpepper's way of getting his own back on Marshal Hammond for being so unfriendly and even threatening towards him. The headline for this piece was, 'A man who knows his duty, even if he is not always able to keep his own house in order'. It read as follows:

On the 29th inst, that well-known lawman, Marshal JEREMIAH HAMMOND of Linton, arrived in our fair city. Many and varied though the attractions of Wichita might be, the marshal's visit to this town was not in the nature of a vacation or pleasure trip. Astounding though it might sound to our readers, Mr HAMMOND had come here hoping to arrest his own daughter: 17 year-old ESTHER. It is rumoured that this young miss, hardly out of the schoolroom, has come to Wichita on an escapade. It is to be hoped that Marshal HAMMOND will not be too hard on the girl once she is recovered and packed off back to her home. The marshal is renowned in his own town for his piety and strict religious observance. It is to be regretted that such an excellent example has not served to keep his own kin on the straight and narrow.

The other article was a little more serious. The headline was:

Victim of knife fight struggles
for life.

Life in the famous cow town of
Delano grows more hazardous by
the day. On Tuesday last, Mr
GROVER McPHERSON, a sol-
dier, became involved in a dispute
with two people near the Lucky
Strike tavern. It is not known what
passed between them, but the
upshot was that Mr McPHERSON
received a serious stab wound to
his back. Authorities at the Sisters
of Mercy Hospital, to which the
injured man was taken, state that
the wound is likely to prove fatal.
An unusual and shocking circumstance surrounding the affair is
that one of those involved is
supposed to be a young woman.

Jeremiah Hammond, who bought the
paper to see if there was anything in it
which might furnish him with a clue as
to his daughter's whereabouts, nearly
had an apoplectic seizure when he read

the bit about himself. He swore to himself that he would visit the offices of the *Wichita Beacon* and wreak vengeance upon the wretched reporter.

Hammond continued to read the rest of the paper and when he came to the piece about the stabbing in Delano, he honestly thought that his heart had stopped beating. He could not have said how he knew, but he was certain that this crime had been committed by his daughter and Chris Turner. He asked a passer-by the location of the Sisters of Mercy Hospital and made his way straight there.

Esther Hammond and Chris Turner were up somewhat earlier than they had been of late and were in an eating house, enjoying a late breakfast. It was eleven in the morning and as they finished their coffee, Esther idly turned the pages of one of the newspapers which the establishment provided for their customers. Her face blanched as she read the first article, that which touched upon her father's arrival in the city. Without a word, she folded the page over and handed it to Chris Turner. 'Shit,' he said coarsely, 'Didn't I just tell you that your father would come looking for us. Shit, that is all we need. Well, there's no hope for it, we must just move to another town.'

'I reckon that you are right,' said Esther irritably. 'He always has to spoil things for me. Even when I leave home, he still has to do it. Why can't he leave me be?' She took the newspaper back from Chris and carried on reading it. When she came to the piece about Grover McPherson, she read it through carefully and then considered whether or not she should tell Chris. In the end, she thought it best to do so. She said quietly, 'Don't holler or anything, but you had best read this as well.' She showed him the piece.

In the cheap novelettes that she read when her father was not around, Esther had often seen it said of this or that person that 'the colour left his face' but never until that moment had she witnessed this event in real life. It was perfectly true though; one moment Chris Turner's healthy and rather unintelligent face had its usual, weathered and ruddy complexion, the next, he was quite literally as white as a sheet of paper. 'Lord,' the girl said to him. 'Don't take on so. We are going to be moving on in any case. It does not signify what happens to that fellow.'

Turner stood up and grabbed Esther by the arm, hustling her out of the eating house. She protested, but for once the boy was not about to be cowed by Marshal Hammond's daughter. He dragged her along the street for a while, until they were altogether out of earshot of anybody else. Then he said to her, 'Esther, do you know what this means? Do you understand what you have done?'

She bridled a little at that and answered, 'You mean, I suppose, what *we* have done, Chris. The two of us were there.'

'If that fellow dies, as the paper says

he is like to, then this will be a hanging matter. We will hang for murder.'

Even then, the girl was not disposed to take quite such a serious and gloomy view of the matter as her friend. 'Well, then maybe he won't die. Anyways, we are going to move to another town, aren't we? There is nothing to connect us with this affair. You worry too much.'

Not for the first time since he had left Linton with her, it struck Chris Turner that there was something missing from Esther's mind. She truly was not quite right in the head. He was a young man who would break rules and take risks, but at least he knew that such things as rules and risks existed and had to be taken into account. Esther did not even seem to be aware of ordinary feelings about such things. That he had become embroiled in what could be a murder was to Chris a terrible thing, partly because the death of a man was a fearful occurrence and in part because his own life might be forfeit as a result. To Esther though, none of this really mattered. Had he but known it, there were learned men who had the very expression to describe such people as Esther Hammond. They called them 'moral defectives' and attributed their unfortunate condition to the ill effects of the way in which they had been raised in childhood.

*   *   *

The Sisters of Mercy Hospital was run by a religious order and the nuns there were pleased to welcome the marshal and offer him every facility. He was taken to what he supposed passed with them for their boss and when he intimated that he had come about Grover McPherson, her face grew grave and she asked him in a hushed voice if he knew that the poor man was not long for this world?

Now Hammond knew that he should at this point have explained his position and made it plain that he had no authority in Wichita. A lie was a lie, whether by commission or omission. He said nothing though and allowed the Sister to believe that he was acting on behalf of the city authorities. He was taken along a corridor to the doctor's office and introduced to that gentleman as a police officer investigating the attack on poor Mr McPherson.

The situation as touched upon the genuine investigation into the stabbing of Grover McPherson may be fairly summed up in a few words: there wasn't one. Fights, rough-houses, beatings, knifings and even shootings were none of them especially uncommon in Delano. The marshal's office took a pragmatic and wholly reprehensible view of such cases, which was that if they involved a respectable citizen of either Wichita or Delano, then they would act as hard as they knew how to nail the culprit. If the victim was some cowboy or drifter from out of town, then they would make one or two initial enquiries, but unless the case could be rapidly solved, they would more or less leave it be.

A deputy had visited the hospital when McPherson was first brought in, but he had been unconscious at that time. A cursory examination of the alley where he had been attacked revealed nothing and nor did speaking to the neighbours shed any light on the case, beyond the fact that a man and woman had been involved. The broken broom handle had not even been noticed, it being assumed that so savage a wound must have been inflicted by something like a Bowie knife.

What Marshal Hammond did not know was that the deputy who had come to enquire after the stabbed man had told the hospital to contact him if McPherson recovered consciousness and was in a fit state to make a statement. When Hammond was ushered into the doctor's office, the doctor took it for granted that he was working for the Wichita office and spoke to him on that basis.

'I was just about to send word to you

people,' said the doctor. 'You wanted to be informed if McPherson came to and he has done so in just the last hour. He is very weak though and so if you are wanting to take a statement, then you had best be quick about it.'

'Meaning, I take it, that he is liable to lapse into unconsciousness again soon?' said Hammond.

'Meaning that he is unlikely to live more than a few hours,' said the doctor. 'His bowel was perforated by whatever weapon was used to stab him. He has galloping septicaemia. In layman's terms: blood poisoning.'

As the doctor took him into the ward to see the dying man, Marshal Hammond knew that despite his fierce adherence to duty, he was in effect perpetrating a fraud here. He was allowing the hospital authorities to think that he was investigating the attack on this man and intending to take a statement which might help find the culprits. Yet he could not for the life of him speak out and disabuse them of this simple misunderstanding. He had become a liar and was also breaking the oath which he took when he had been sworn in as a marshal.

Grover McPherson looked awful. His skin was like yellow parchment and his breathing rapid, as though the air was not entering his lungs properly. You did not need to be a doctor to see that he was in a bad way and probably not apt to live beyond that day. The doctor felt his pulse and then caught Hammond's eye and shook his head slightly.

McPherson's eyes were closed and the doctor leaned over him and said, 'Mr McPherson, you have a visitor from the marshal's office.'

The man in the bed opened his eyes and appeared to be having trouble focussing. He said, in a thin, reedy voice, not at all what one would expect for a man with such a large and solid frame, 'I don't feel too good, doc. Can you give me something for the pain?'

'Yes, just talk to the marshal here and I will fetch something for you.' He patted the man's arm in a helpless way.

'Hallo, Mr McPherson,' said Hammond, 'I am a marshal and I was wondering if you could tell me about the people who did this to you?'

'A boy jumped me. I went to take a leak in an alley and this kid pushed me and tried to take my wallet.'

'I see. What happened next? Did he stab you?'

'No,' said McPherson. 'That was the strangest thing. I was able to handle the boy. I got him in a bear-hug. I might have been liquored up, but I was still able to handle a kid like him.' The effort of talking seemed to have exhausted the man, because his breathing was even more laboured and he closed his eyes as though he wished to rest. The compassionate thing to do would surely be to leave him in peace, but Hammond had to know the truth about this. He shook McPherson's shoulder roughly and said, 'Well, how did you come to be stabbed?'

The dying man opened his eyes again

76

and said, 'It was the girl. I saw her come up behind me. She did me from behind. Then when I fell down, she said, 'Get his wallet, Chris.' That's all I remember.'

At this point, the doctor returned with a syringe. He said to Hammond, 'Have you found out all that you wished to know? If so, then I think that it would be a kindness to let this poor fellow sleep.'

'Yes,' said Hammond, distractedly. 'Yes, of course.'

When he had left the hospital, the marshal was in such a state of fearful anxiety that he scarcely knew where he was going. He walked out towards the river-front and just stood there staring. As soon as that poor, wretched man had said the name 'Chris', Hammond had known that his worst fears were realized and that his own daughter had done murder. For there seemed little doubt that although the man was still breathing now, he would like as not be dead by the end of the day. That at least was what he had collected from all that the doctor had said.

This changed everything forever; his life, both as a father and as a law man, was ended this day. How could he continue, knowing that he had raised a murderer and also conspired to pervert the course of justice by representing himself at the hospital as having come to gather evidence to track down a killer? For Marshal Hammond knew very well that despite all his piety and faith, there was not the slightest chance that he would help to deliver his own daughter to the hangman. Even if it mean fighting against and betraying all that he had ever held dear to him, yes even the Lord Jesus himself, he would move heaven and earth to protect his only child from the consequences of her rash and foolish actions.

As marshal, Jeremiah Hammond had attended a number of hangings, although thankfully never that of a woman. Each one of them had been as ghastly an event as could be conceived in the worst nightmare and it was only his fixed conviction that this was what justice required which made him able to play his part in the process. Now, thinking of Esther being led to the gallows and executed made him feel quite literally sick with horror. He knew then that whatever it might take, he would act to prevent such a thing happening.

Coming here to Wichita, he had only meant to drag his daughter back home and perhaps see her set up in a court and reprimanded for being present at a theft. Now that she faced the possibility of execution the marshal would take all necessary steps, bar none, to save her from death.

★ ★ ★

Chris could not sit still for more than a minute at a time. There was hardly enough space to take two paces in the room where he and Esther were staying, but even so he kept jumping up and peering wildly out of the window, as though he expected at any moment to see the hangman approaching to lead him to the gallows. He was so distracted with fear that Esther could see that it was she who would need to make any arrangement to take them to the safety of another town.

'I am going down to the railroad station,' said Esther, 'The sooner we leave here, the better, I would say.'

'Don't go just yet, Esther.'

'I can't stay in here with you. You are driving me crazy with your restlessness. Nobody has tied us in with that man. I have thrown the wallet in the river and all that remains is the money. There is nothing to fear.'

'Don't you care about him, Esther? Does it matter to you, what we have done? He might have had a wife, children. Now he is dying because of what we done.'

'No, I can't say that I am much worried about him,' said the girl frankly. 'See, I never knew him. He is nothing to me.'

'I am not like you. I felt bad when I had hit that fellow at the depot back in Linton. I would not have done that without your urging. This is ten times, a hundred times worse. I don't know if I can carry on, bearing the burden of it, like.'

'Well you had best carry on,' Esther said, giving the boy a sharp look. 'If not, then I do not know what will befall us.'

'Just set here with me for a spell,' said Chris Turner. 'I will be ready to take action by and by, but for now I durst not go out into the street.'

Esther pulled an impatient face and said, 'Well mind that you buck up your ideas a bit, otherwise we are going to be in trouble.'

Just across the river from where the two young people were staying, Marshal Hammond stood staring right at the building, had his daughter and her friend but known it. He was trying to put his thoughts in some sort of order and work out firstly what he *should* do and then after that, what he actually was going to be doing. Really, he already knew the answers to both questions, but these were so much at odds with his principles and religious convictions that he was hoping that everything might change if he only stood there long enough.

While he stood there, his mind working frantically and to no good purpose, Hammond became aware that a small group of people seemed to have come and stood right alongside him. Since the riverside was practically deserted, this was a little annoying and he began to feel crowded. He needed to move about a bit anyway; he had been standing there for the better part of half an hour, just gazing out across the water. He turned to move off and found his way blocked by four young men. They were the cowboys with whom he had had the run-in on the train from Linton and it looked very much as though they had recognized him and were desirous of talking over what had happened on the last occasion that they had chanced to meet Jeremiah Hammond.

5

The young men had recognized Hammond from behind, but it was not until he turned to leave that the full state of affairs was revealed to them. Their intention up to this point had been simply to rough him up a bit in order to punish him for the way that he had humiliated two of their party a few days previously. The two whom he had assaulted felt very bitter about their experience and had already more than once reproached their friends for not setting upon on the fellow who had attacked them. When Marshal Hammond turned around and faced them though, it looked as though the case was altered.

For one thing, the target of the boys wrath had not been wearing a tin star when last they encountered him. They still had him pegged for a preacher of some sort, albeit a very forceful and aggressive specimen of the breed. The discovery that the man with whom they had tangled and with whom they now purposed to try conclusions was a marshal was one unexpected development. Hand in hand with this first surprise went another: that the fellow that they hoped to knock about a bit was carrying a gun.

The marshal, who was feeling more sad than he had ever been in his life, looked at the four boys and saw immediately what they wanted. He said, 'Well, you fellows obviously have it in mind to start a fight with me. I tell you now, that I wish for nothing of the sort. I have much to do and if you just leave me be, then I will not trouble you.'

For a few seconds, it looked as though this might be sufficient to avert the violence which had been threatened. The two young men who had not been assaulted by Marshal Hammond stood undecided, as did the fellow he had grabbed by the throat. This was not so for the man who had lost two teeth when Hammond had landed a blow in his mouth. He had a particular grudge against the older man, a grudge which he was determined should be settled there and then.

'Will you set to with me, man to man and forgetting that you are the law?' said the boy.

'Lord knows, I do not wish to,' said the marshal, 'but you have every right to ask it of me. So yes, if that is what you will.'

'You're damned right, I will,' said the cowboy.

'You other men, now,' said Hammond, 'I suppose that you do not intend to fall upon me if I set aside my gun and fight your partner here?'

The other three shrugged and shook their heads. Just a few minutes ago, they had been on the point of jumping this fellow, but since he had shown himself decent enough to offer satisfaction to the man who felt aggrieved, they would have thought it cowardly and unmanly to take advantage of the situation.

It was a chilly day, but without further ado, Hammond removed his jacket and unbuckled his gunbelt. Then he took off his hat, rolled up his sleeves and prepared for combat. The setup was a novel one and not wholly to the liking of the boy who had been so keen to lay into Hammond as part of a group. He had already received proof of the marshal's physical prowess and was not at all sure that he was ready for the return match. There was, however, no way of backing out of the business now without becoming the butt of his friends' jokes and so he too stripped down to his shirtsleeves and readied himself for the fight.

At first sight, all the advantages were with the young cowboy. He was half Hammond's age, physically as fit as could be and possessed of a mean and vengeful disposition into the bargain. However, the marshal was the more experienced fighter who knew one or two tricks in that line and had never given up in a physical contest in his life. His tenacity and staying power were assets which had in the past outweighed the brute strength and viciousness of various opponents.

Many fist fights between men are almost of a symbolic nature. One man rushes the other and overwhelms his defences, whereupon the weaker man capitulates and acknowledges the other to be his superior. They are like contests between males proving that they are leaders of the pack in the animal kingdom. None of this had any bearing at all on the way that Jeremiah Hammond comported himself in a fight. The younger man on this occasion rushed Hammond and delivered a furious hail of blows upon his head and upper body. Instead of falling back in the traditional manner, the marshal stood his ground and waited until the cowboy's energy was dissipated. Then he responded with two or three strong punches of his own to the man's face.

A thing that the other three men

observed was that while their friend hopped and danced around Marshal Hammond, the older man stood there like a tree, saving the whole of his strength to use in punches aimed at vulnerable parts of the other man's anatomy. He received blows to his own body, but seemed to ignore them. The consequence was that rather than being over in a few seconds of furious action, the fight between the two men looked set to last for some time. Various loafers caught sight of something happening on the grass by the riverside and drifted over to form a ring of spectators. It was this which attracted the attention of Deputy Pete Atkins as he rode by on other business. He was in something of a hurry, but even so, he could hardly ignore disorderly conduct of this kind.

So engrossed were they in the fight, that nobody noticed Deputy Atkins ride up and dismount. One or two of the more enterprising of the onlookers had started a book on the fight, both of them giving odds in favour of Marshal

Hammond's eventual victory.

'Come along now, you men,' came the voice of the deputy. 'Break it up now. What the Devil do you mean by brawling in this way in public? I have places in the cells for those who disturb the peace in this fashion.'

Atkins stopped dead and fell silent when he recognized one of the combatants as the marshal of Linton. The crowd melted away, leaving only the two men who had been fighting and the other three cowboys. Pete Atkins shook his head in disbelief. 'This won't do at all,' he said. 'What has been happening here?'

The four young men looked to be lost for words and so Hammond spoke up. 'I had some species of dispute with this young fellow on the train from Linton. He wished for satisfaction and I offered it to him. I am sorry to occasion a breach of the peace in this way, but the fault is mine and not his. I should know better.'

His manly bearing and readiness to

shoulder the blame for the incident greatly impressed the four young men. Hammond turned to the boy with whom he had been scrapping and offered his hand, saying, 'Sorry son, I hope that we might part on good terms?'

The two men shook hands, at which point Deputy Atkins said harshly, 'All right you four, get along out of here now. And no more fighting, you hear what I tell you?'

When the other men had left, Atkins said to Marshal Hammond, 'I am surprised at you, you know. I would not have expected a man like you to be brawling in public.'

'Yes,' said Hammond. 'You speak fairly. I am sorry. I am distracted by recent events and am not thinking straight.'

The deputy decided to let the matter lie. He said, 'Fact is, I was in search of you and am pleased to have found you now. I went by Chang's place looking for you, but he did not know where you were to be found. I wonder you don't mind staying with an old humbug like him.'

'I like Mr Chang and I think that his view on many topics is perfectly correct,' said Hammond a little stiffly.

Pete Atkins looked at the man sidewise, taken aback by this statement. When he had been in Linton the previous year, Marshal Hammond's detestation of any religion apart from the true one which he himself professed was universally remarked upon. He limited himself to observing, 'You are becoming more liberal perhaps than was once the case.'

A few days earlier, a remark of this nature would have been enough to set Jeremiah Hammond's hackles on end, but today he simply said in a tired and dispirited way, 'That is nothing to the purpose. What was it that you wanted to speak to me about?' He had a grim foreboding that the deputy was about to tell him either that his daughter had been taken up on a charge of murder or that his own role in suppressing the evidence of a dying man had been discovered. It was somewhat of a relief to learn that it was neither of these things.

'I will tell you how it is, Marshal Hammond. My boss is out of town for a while and there is only me and two other men running the show here. A young woman was taken advantage of last night and also badly beaten. We know, or leastways, have a strong suspicion who is responsible for the crime and now have to apprehend him.'

'Forgive me, Atkins, but could I ask you to tell me where I enter the picture? I have no authority in this town and am here solely in pursuit of a fugitive.'

'I am coming to that. The young man wanted for the attack on this girl, who by the by is only fifteen and entirely respectable, is a fellow called Clint Barker. He lives with his father and four other brothers out about seven or eight miles from here. The father and all five of his boys are the meanest and most vicious crew you could hope to meet. They have all run foul of the law more than once and they live in a farmhouse which could be defended against a small army.'

'I am reminded of Proverbs ten, verse nineteen,' said Hammond with a rare flash of humour. '"In the multitude of words, there wanteth not sin." You have yet to reach your point, though you have spoken many words.'

'Well, in short, I need more than just me and the other two deputies to go out and arrest Clint Barker. There is no enthusiasm for any sort of posse and I wondered if you would care to lend a hand?'

It might have been thought that, bowed down as he was with his fears for the fate of his daughter and the way in which he had himself strayed from the right path, Marshal Hammond would have rejected such an idea as this out of hand. However, just as with his recent fight with the young cowboy, such an affair promised to take his mind away

94

from his own troubles and so he said, 'If I can be back here by nightfall, then yes, I don't mind. I have no horse with me, mind.'

'That's nothing,' said Atkins. 'We can find a mount for you. I will ride back to the office and make arrangements. Will you follow on foot?'

'Yes, yes I will.'

*   *   *

The best thing that Esther Hammond could have done, given the unfortunate circumstances in which she found herself, would have been to sit quietly in the room with Chris Turner and keep out of public sight. Such a course of action did not at all accord with her desires. It was to avoid being trapped indoors during the day that she had run off from her home in Linton. She was not about to trade one sort of imprisonment for another. So it was that when Turner fell into a fitful sleep, tormented by dreams of the hangman's rope, the girl slipped out of the cheap hotel so that she could get some fresh air. In her purse, she carried two $100 bills from the wallet of the man whom she and Turner had robbed. The bulk of Grover McPherson's money had consisted of eight $100 notes: this being the money which he had won at the faro table the night that he was attacked and mortally wounded. There had been a little over ten dollars in small change, but the young couple had now spent that.

Had she been a little older or perhaps more versed in the ways of the world, it might have occurred to Esther Hammond that for a young girl to offer a $100 bill in a store would invite attention. As it was, she had led a sheltered life and seldom been called upon to handle money. Her aunt had seen to the shopping and suchlike and her father had not approved of the idea of giving children an allowance or 'pocket money'.

Although she was not in the pitiful

state that Chris Turner was, Esther still had the idea that her mood might perhaps be improved by a couple of glasses of whiskey. She had begun to drink secretly around six or nine months ago, meeting at odd times with a bunch of youngsters who were, like her, determined to defy their parents. Then, on arriving in Wichita, she had been drinking in saloons each day. Never yet though had she thought of having a whole, entire bottle of intoxicating liquor for her own self.

The store sold all sorts of things, from lamp oil to bolts of cloth. The only thing that interested Esther though was a shelf high up behind the counter, lined up on which were bottles of spirits, chiefly whiskey. She found the notion of buying a bottle of whiskey quite alarming, but so strong was her desire for the effects of a few drinks that she overcame her initial reluctance and, waiting until there were no other customers waiting to be served, went up to the clerk behind the counter.

'Say, could you give me a bottle of that whiskey?' she asked. The clerk looked at her oddly and Esther wondered if she should first have asked how much it was.

She felt herself reddening, which caused the man behind the counter to ask, 'Are you of age?'

'I am twenty-one, yes,' she replied boldly. He looked as though he did not believe her but reached up anyway for the whiskey.

'That will be one dollar and sixty cents, please.' said the clerk. His eyes widened in disbelief at the $100 bill which Esther produced. 'I can't change that, miss. I will need something smaller.'

Esther began to grow confused and the shop man suddenly reached over and snatched the bill from her hands. 'I am not stealing this from you,' he told her, 'but something is not right here. How come a girl like you has half a year's salary in her hands? I shall send my boy to the marshal's office and they will look into the matter.'

The frightened girl knew that she had to get out of there before any lawman came enquiring about the source of her wealth and so without more ado, she bolted from the store, hearing the man shouting for her to stop as she ran into the street.

When he got back to the office after having enlisted Jeremiah Hammond's aid in the projected visit to the Barker place, Pete Atkins found that Culpepper was hanging around and shooting the breeze with Dave Fletcher, another of the deputies. Pete said, 'Jed, you will catch it damned hot if you are still here five minutes from now. Marshal Hammond is on his way here and I do not think he is best pleased at seeing that bit of yours about him and his daughter in the paper.' None of that was true, but Atkins wanted to be able to plan how to go about bringing in Clint Barker without having the fear that Barker would read of their plans in the Wichita Beacon before ever they arrived at his father's farm. The reporter took the hint and made himself scarce.

After the newspaperman had gone, Fletcher said, 'So Hammond agreed to throw in with us and ride up to get Barker? That's good of him; he doesn't need to help like that.'

'He's not himself,' said Atkins. 'I tell you, I have seen him before in Linton and heard a deal about him. He is reckoned to be the coldest man alive, but do you know what he was about when I ran him to earth down by the river?'

'No, go on.'

'He was engaged in a fist fight with some cowboy. Just fighting in public.'

'Was he trying to arrest him?'

'No,' said Atkins. 'He was just fighting. I tell you, there is something troubling that man.'

'It probably concerns his daughter. I could not believe it when I heard about that warrant for her that he had sworn out. He is a strange one all right.'

Ten minutes later, the man himself

arrived at the office and plans were laid for the arrest of Clint Barker.

The gelding that Pete Atkins had secured for him was a mite too skittish for Marshal Hammond's tastes. Every minute or two, the creature would take it into its head to take a few paces sideways, like it was practising dressage or something of that sort. The first few times it happened, Hammond ignored it, but when it became clear that this was a regular vice, he cracked down on the horse and was pretty firm whenever he detected it in the act. If there was going to be any chance of gunplay or rough stuff, then the marshal wanted a beast that he could rely upon, not one that might unexpectedly bolt and take him into the line of fire.

* * *

Ethan Barker and his five sons lived in a stone-built farmhouse which sat perched on top of a rise of ground. The mother of the boys had dug up and left some ten years before, leaving the old man to raise his sons as best he was able. The rumour in town was that his wife had finally had enough of the vicious beatings that Ethan Barker dished out when he was in his cups. Whether or not that was the reason, there was now just the five men living in the house.

Ethan and the five 'boys', who ranged in age from nineteen to twenty six, had all been in trouble with the law on many occasions. If it wasn't distilling and selling moonshine liquor, it was selling guns in the Indian Territories. There was usually at least one or two of them in gaol and it was very rare for all five to be living in the old house, as was presently the case. Clint, who was twenty four, was said to be the meanest of the bunch and this was not the first time that he had been in trouble for knocking women about. Beating up a child of fifteen was bad though, even for him.

Marshal Hammond and the two

deputies from Wichita sat on their horses watching the smoke trickle up from the chimney into the still autumn air. 'Well,' said Pete Atkins. 'They look to be at home.'

'Some of them are, at any rate,' said the more cautious Hammond. 'We need to recollect that while we are coming at the house from this direction, we could find some of them boys coming up behind us. We do not want to be caught between the hammer and the anvil, as you might say.'

Marshal Hammond had not been displeased to be roped into a game of this kind. At least while he was fooling around like this, he did not have time to brood upon the business about his daughter.

The two younger deputies seemed inclined to give way to him in the matter of tactics, notwithstanding where this was more properly their home territory than it was his. Hammond said, 'Well, how do you boys want to play it?'

'Me and Fletcher were wondering,' said Atkins. 'How you would yourself play it, if you were in charge, that is to say?'

'That is a hard question to gauge, seeing that I do not know the men. How apt are they to cut up rough if we knock on the door and demand that they hand over this Clint?'

'They are every one of them as tough as all-get-out-and-push,' said Fletcher. 'They might very well refuse to deliver the boy up to us or even start shooting if they have been drinking.'

'Still and all,' said Hammond. 'We cannot just act as though we are besieging the house. We must give them a chance to play the game by the rules. I will go up and knock on the door.'

It was clear that both Atkins and Fletcher felt uncomfortable about this suggestion, less because they particularly wished to march up to the front door of the Barker place than because it made them look cowardly. 'I am not sure,' said Atkins. 'Strikes me that as senior deputy, that is more my job.'

Jeremiah Hammond shrugged. 'Just as you like. I am happy to do it. I don't think they will gun down a man like that, just for knocking on the door.'

'If you're sure,' said Atkins.

'Sure, I'm sure.' Marshal Hammond walked the horse up the slope towards the front of the house. When he was thirty feet from it, he reined in the animal and called out in a loud voice, 'You men in there! We are peace officers and have come to arrest one Clint Barker. Send him out now.'

There was no response. Then two things happened, one very quickly after the other. The first was that his horse skittered sideways, as it had been doing at intervals all the way out here. A fraction of a second later, somebody opened up with a rifle from the upper story of the farmhouse and even as he spurred on the horse, Hammond thought that if the creature had not moved to one side, then that bullet would very likely have struck him. By the time that he had rejoined the other two men at the foot of the hill, Marshal Hammond knew that he had had an exceedingly lucky escape.

'Why, those murderous rogues,' said Pete Atkins. 'If that horse of yours hadn't jittered at just that moment, I mind that you would have stopped a bullet there.'

'The same thought had also crossed my mind,' said Hammond drily. 'I vote that we should not let the men in that house get away with this. It sets the law at nought and gives wicked men an altogether wrong idea of their place in the scheme of things.'

'I am with you there. I will not leave here without making at least one arrest and perhaps more,' said Atkins.

'I have been looking closely at the structure of yon house,' said the marshal, 'There are windows at the front and I dare say also at the back. Is that right?'

Fletcher said, 'Yeah, there are as

many at the back as there are at the front.'

'But not at the sides of the building,' said Hammond. 'They are just plain stone. I think that if a man were to approach the place from one of those blind sides, then he might be able to get right up close to the house, especially if a couple of other men kept the occupants of the house busy by firing at them.'

6

Getting up to the side wall of the Barkers' farmhouse had not been a particularly difficult enterprise, with Fletcher and Atkins keeping up a pretty regular fire to stop those in the house from looking out of the windows too freely. Having gained the side of the house, Hammond then had to work out his next move. Since the action all seemed to be focused at the front of the place, it seemed to him to make sense if he were to creep round the back and see what was what.

Very few people will bother keeping the back door of a farmhouse locked and bolted during the daytime. Marshal Hammond therefore peered round the side of the house and then dropped to his hands and knees. In this way, he crawled past the rear windows unseen until he gained the door. Carefully, and being sure to make no rattling noise, he grasped the handle of the door and turned it very slowly. He then pushed the door inwards slightly, until he had established to his own satisfaction that it was neither locked nor bolted. Then he pulled it to again and allowed the door handle to return to its usual position.

Jeremiah Hammond crouched for a moment or two by the back door, considering whether it would be better to charge in with his pistol blazing, or if it would make more sense to tip-toe in and try to take the men from behind, unawares. In the end, he decided that this course of action was the one to favour and so, drawing and cocking his pistol, he again turned the door handle with agonizing slowness and then swung open the door. He stood up and looked into the kitchen, but could see nobody. Hammond slipped into the house and closed the back door gently behind him.

All the time, the shooting was

continuing sporadically, from both inside and outside the house. Marshal Hammond moved softly through the ground floor rooms of the house, without encountering anybody. He went into a large room at the front of the house and then cautiously approached the window. He had no wish to be shot by the deputies who still maintained an intermittent fusillade. He waved to the two deputies, who he could just see sheltering behind a pile of logs down the slope a ways. Once he was sure that they had seen him and were likely to hold fire for a bit, he made his way up the stairs.

'What do you think?' said Atkins. 'He is in the house now. Should we just crouch here while he does all the work?'

He and Fletcher had stopped firing and the shooting from the house also appeared to have ceased. Dave Fletcher said, 'Truth to tell, I feel mean staying here while Hammond runs the risks. What say that we charge to the house? I think that if Hammond is about to tackle those who have been firing at us, then he will need our help in distracting them.'

'You are right,' said Pete Atkins. 'Let's go now.' The two of them jumped up and began running towards the house. They zigzagged as they went, but there did not look to be any need. Nobody fired at them. Half way up the slope, they heard the crack of pistol shots from within the house. The two deputies put on a spurt and ran even faster towards the front door of the farmhouse.

The door was unlocked and Fletcher and Atkins charged into the house and ran straight up the stairs. They almost shot Jeremiah Hammond, who they met coming down towards them. 'Well, man,' said Atkins. 'What's the score? What has chanced?'

'There were two men up there,' said Hammond. 'I have shot them both and they are dead.' He led the others to a front bedroom, where Ethan Barker and his youngest son were sprawled lifeless upon the floor. Both men had been shot through the head and by each corpse lay a rifle. 'Is either of these the man you sought?' asked Marshal Hammond.

'No, this is the father and that there is Jake, his youngest boy,' said Atkins.

'Why the hell would they shoot at us?' asked Fletcher, perplexed. 'They must have known that Clint would not be likely to spend more than a few months in gaol for what he did.'

Hammond indicated some large glass containers in the corner of the room. 'I will hazard a guess and say that they had been imbibing freely of illicitly distilled spirits.' He went over and picked up one of the jars, holding it up to his nose and sniffing. 'Yes, I should think that the two of them had been drinking this stuff heavily. I dare say that they knew that we would be coming for that fellow Clint and just hoped to drive us off by a few shots.'

Pete Atkins went over to the bodies and knelt beside them. 'They both reek of poteen. I think you have the case pretty well figured out, Hammond. I wonder where the other four boys are to be found.'

'Then I guess we ought to look around and see if your man is hiding out anywhere,' said Hammond. They all went downstairs into the kitchen and Pete Atkins opened the kitchen door, coming face to face in the process with Clint Barker. Barker, who had been down in one of the fields, hearing the gunfire, had come running back to the house. He looked as surprised to see Atkins as Atkins was to bump like this into the man he was seeking. It was a close thing as to which of the two men recovered first from his surprise and took action.

As the deputy brought up his pistol, Clint Barker drew his as fast as a bolt of lightning and shot the other man dead on the spot. When the bullet hit him in the chest, Atkins said, 'Oh!' as naturally as if he had just remembered something that he needed to do. Then he dropped lifeless to the kitchen floor. Almost immediately, Fletcher fired at the man who had killed his partner and Clint Barker too, fell dead.

Marshal Hammond and Deputy Fletcher tried to revive Atkins, but it was a hopeless endeavour. The bullet had passed clean through his heart and he must have been dead before he even fell. The plan had been for a simple and uncomplicated arrest of a man for an offence which might at worst have drawn him six months in gaol and now four men were dead. It was, thought Hammond, a dreadful end to the day. He had only known Atkins for a short time, but had liked what he saw. It was a senseless waste of a good man's life.

Fletcher and Hammond laid Pete Atkins carefully over his horse, with a view to taking his body back to town. The three Barkers they decided to leave where they were for the time being.

As they rode back to Wichita, Marshal Hammond reflected that this would make it even less likely that anybody would be prosecuting any serious enquiry into the attack on Grover McPherson. He felt ashamed of himself for even thinking such a thing, but he could not help being a little glad that this business would serve to put further distance between the crime which his daughter had committed in this town. With their own marshal still out of town and only two deputies now to look after law and order in the town, Hammond could not see that anybody would even remember the McPherson case in another week.

When they got back to the office, Fletcher said to the marshal, 'I appreciate what you done for us, back there. You are not to blame for Pete's death. I need to rouse up the other deputy, who must be told that he must come on duty right this minute. Could I ask you to mind the office for a space, while I take Pete to the undertaker and find Jack Seagrove?'

'You go along, son. I will set here until you return. Do not hurry yourself,

115

I know how to run an office of this sort; don't you fret about that.'

'Lord knows what we would have done without you,' said Fletcher and left the office. Ten minutes after Fletcher left, a middle-aged man walked through the door and said to Hammond, 'I have some evidence as might touch upon the robbery and knifing of that poor fellow the other night.'

It was obvious that this man assumed that Marshal Hammond was the duly appointed authority in charge of the office, which in a sense was exactly right. He did not look for Fletcher to return in under an hour and so the trick of the thing was to find out how much this man knew about the attack in which Esther had been involved and then work out how to get him to keep his mouth shut. This was not how Hammond put the case of course, not even to his own self, but this was without doubt the substance of the matter.

'Come in and sit down,' said the marshal, welcomingly. 'Tell me what you know about the case.'

Like so many law abiding people who seldom have dealings with the police, the man who gave his name as Harry Hawkins was ill at ease in the marshal's office. 'I am not accusing anybody mind,' said Hawkins, 'and likewise, I hope that nobody will accuse me of anything if I am wrong.'

'What could anybody accuse you of, Mr Hawkins?' asked Hammond.

'Why, of stealing a hundred dollars,' he answered anxiously.

Slowly and patiently, Marshal Hammond drew out of the storekeeper the whole story of how the young girl had come in to buy whiskey and how she had run off when challenged and left him holding the $100 bill. Hawkins was most particularly concerned to hand this over to the authorities. He had heard from friends who frequented the Lucky Strike that the man who had been attacked and robbed had had a series of good wins at the table there and was supposed to have been carrying almost a thousand dollars when he left. For this reason, and bearing in mind what the newspaper said about a young woman being implicated, Mr Hawkins had been suspicious of the £100 bill being offered like that. Anyways, he hoped that he had done his duty now.

Jeremiah Hammond felt weak with relief that it had been he who was sitting here and taking down this statement and not one of the Wichita deputies. He was a shrewd judge of character and it was his considered opinion that Mr Harry Hawkins had never seen the inside of the marshal's office before and would most likely go the rest of his life without setting foot in the place after this day. After taking the $100 bill into safe keeping, getting Mr Hawkins to sign a statement and then finding out the precise location of his store, the marshal shook the man's hand and thanked him profusely for being such a good citizen. Hawkins' detailed description of the girl who had tried to pass the bill could only be of Esther.

'If only there were more people like you around, Mr Hawkins,' said Hammond. 'It gladdens my heart and restores my faith in human nature. There is one final point though and that is this. Our investigation into this case is at a very delicate point and if anybody heard anything about this incident which you have reported, it could wreck the whole of the investigation. I must ask you to promise that you will not breathe a word of this to a living soul. I know that you are a decent man and do not want any trouble with the law.'

The slight menace of the final sentence was, Hammond guessed, going to be enough to ensure that the man kept his mouth shut.

When Hawkins had gone, Marshal Hammond rooted around the office until he found a street map of the city, a map which included Delano. He marked the site of the attack on Grover McPherson and then added a cross for the site of Harry Hawkins' store. Then, as an afterthought, he also put in a mark to show where the Lucky Strike saloon was to be found. I just know, he thought to himself, that Esther is hiding somewhere near those three spots.

By the time that Fletcher got back, it was dark. Hammond had a very clear view of what was needful for him to do now. Before heading for Delano though, he thought that it would do no harm at all to visit the Sisters of Mercy Infirmary again. He got there forty minutes after Grover McPherson died of blood poisoning.

'Ah, Marshal Hammond,' said the doctor, when he caught sight of the marshal in a corridor. 'You seem to a have a knack of turning up at crucial moments. First you arrive just as the patient came to, and now you come here just after he dies.'

The doctor took Hammond to a

small room, hardly bigger than a large closet, which functioned as the mortuary. 'Do you want me to go over the cause of death?'

'No,' said Hammond. 'That seems fairly straightforward. It was a stab wound from behind which caused a fatal infection of the blood. Would that about be the case in brief?'

'Yes, pretty well. What do you wish us to do with the corpse?'

'What is the usual procedure when some indigent dies in your hospital? Who arranges the burial?'

'We do. Then we bill the city afterwards. I thought it might be different in this case though, because of the circumstances of the death.'

'No,' said Marshal Hammond casually. 'You can go right ahead and fix up the burial. Then just send in the bill as usual.'

The doctor did not appear to find anything odd about Hammond's instructions, merely nodding and indicating that he would see to it. For a man who had always stuck to the rules with an almost fanatical rigidity, Jeremiah Hammond was finding it amazingly easy to twist, bend and break those selfsame rules now that he had a strong motive for doing so. And really, no motive could be more powerful than to protect his young daughter from suffering a painful and degrading public death at the hands of the hangman.

* * *

It was astonishing how readily people trusted a marshal and answered the questions that he put to them with no apparent hesitation. Perhaps the fact that the management of the Lucky Strike were especially anxious to stay on the right side of the law had some bearing on their willingness to cooperate. They knew that if they crossed the marshal's office or failed to provide enough information, then there would be all sorts of difficulties when their gambling licence came up for renewal.

'I am investigating a crime,' said the marshal. 'It is a complicated financial matter and I cannot say too much about it. I am sure that you will understand my discretion.'

The under manager to whom he spoke, had not the least idea what Marshal Hammond meant, but he nodded his head vigorously to show how keen he was to help.

'Tell me,' continued Hammond. 'Have you had a young woman, barely more than a girl really, in here lately who fits this description?' He gave a brief word portrait of his daughter and could tell at once that the man knew the girl.

'When you say that she was little more than a girl,' said the deputy manager of the Lucky Strike, 'I hope that this has no reference to our serving minors with intoxicating liquor or allowing them to gamble? We are right strict about this here, but short of asking to see birth documents and such, there is little we can do to stamp out that evil.' The man suspected, quite correctly, that it might sound as though he was overdoing his virtuous indignation about under-age drinking. If so, the marshal standing opposite him did not appear to note the fact.

'To speak bluntly, Mr Trelawny, I don't care about the serving of under-age patrons with alcohol,' said Hammond and marvelled that he could make such a statement without dying of shame. 'I want only to find this young person.'

'Well then, she came in with a man every night for close to a week. I am pretty well sure that this was the girl, I mean woman, who you described.'

'What did she and her companion do here?'

The man looked puzzled and wondered what the marshal thought that young folk generally did in a saloon or gambling house. 'Well,' he said. 'They played a little faro and imbibed a certain quantity of whiskey. Not to the point of intoxication, you understand, we never allow that.'

Jeremiah Hammond was not over-fond of saloon keepers at the best of times and right now he was in a hurry. He moved a little closer to Roland Trelawny and said quietly, 'Mr Trelawny, you have a choice. You can tell me just exactly what I wish to know, in which case I give you my oath that I shall leave here and never set mind to you or your establishment again. Or you can stand there and fox with me, wasting my time with a lot of nonsense and lies. If you take that road, then I will do my damnedest to make your life a burden. I will try to have this pesthole closed down and you thrown out of work. After that, I will hound you until you have to move to another town. Now make up your mind which you would have, I am in a hurry.'

Having the case presented to him in this concise and unambiguous way focused the manager's mind in a marvellous way and also loosened his tongue. He said, 'The girl that you talk of was a bad one. She was drinking, using foul language and encouraging the young man with her to all manner of foolishness. People complained about her conduct and she was warned on more than one occasion that she was coming close to being thrown out.'

'Did she look to you to be acting under coercion? By which I mean, was the young man ordering her about?'

Trelawny gave a short laugh. 'As to that, I would say that the boot was all on the other foot. Struck me that he was a weak-willed kind of boy and that she was pulling his strings, as they say. No sir, she was the strong one there and no mistake.'

'There now,' said the marshal. 'That was not too hard, was it? When last did you see her in here?'

'Couple of nights ago.'

'Thank you kindly for your help, Mr Trelawny. There is one last thing.' Hammond moved even closer to the man. 'If I hear that anybody under the age of twenty-one is ever served liquor in this place again, I will have you locked up. Is that understood?'

The deputy manager of the Lucky Strike nodded. This was the sort of thing that he understood very well.

★ ★ ★

Esther had expected Chris to be furious about the loss of the $100 bill to the man in the store, but he hardly seemed to care about it at all. He said in a dull voice, like he was not really paying attention, 'Gee, that's a shame.' But beyond that, he did not mention the matter again. There was a weary and dispirited air about him which Esther found a little worrying. She wondered if he was sickening for something. All he wanted was to stay in the room and lay on the bed, staring blankly up at the ceiling.

'Chris,' said the girl to him, 'we need to make our plans. Recollect that we are going to get a train west soon. How are we to break one of those $100 notes if we are viewed with such suspicion as soon as we present them?'

'I don't know, Esther,' Turner told her. 'I don't think that I ever had more than five dollars in my life before meeting you. It is not a problem that has ever faced me before.'

'Ah, you're no use to me sometimes, Chris Turner, you know that? I thought that you would be fun to go off with, but I would have had more high jinks with your kid sister!'

Turner did not even have the strength to be annoyed at Esther for twitting him in this way. All he could think of since he heard about the man they had robbed being at the point of death, was the likelihood of his answering for the crime on the scaffold. Nothing else mattered in the least. His only wish, and a right fervent one at that, was that he would wake up at his mother's house and find that all this had been a bad dream.

128

For Marshal Hammond's daughter, the death of a stranger was not something which concerned her much. She did not have any vivid memory of sticking that piece of wood through his back and even if she could have remembered the incident clearly, it is to be feared that what passed for a conscience with her would not have been troubled.

Right from her earliest childhood, virtue for Esther had meant concealing wrongdoing from others, chiefly her father. That one would choose to do good for the sake of it had never once crossed her mind. Hers was a most practical system of ethics, in which right behaviour might lead to praise from those around one and eventually a place in heaven. Unacceptable conduct had therefore to be hidden away and, if nobody knew of it, then it could safely be forgotten. Incredible to relate, stabbing a man to death had been banished to that far corner of her mind where she was accustomed to thrust minor peccadillos like raiding the cookie jar.

* * *

After speaking to the fellow at The Lucky Strike, Marshal Hammond explored the streets surrounding the saloon, paying particular attention to those in the direction of the store where his daughter had tried to pass the large bill and also those near to the place where Grover McPherson had been set upon. He had not the remotest doubt now that Esther was staying nearby with that wretched boy Chris Turner. It was getting late and he determined to make a thorough and systematic search of every likely place where the young people might be holed up, first thing in the morning.

Hammond thought it fitting to return to the office before retiring for the night, in order to condole with Dave Fletcher, who had lost his friend and partner that day. He directed his steps towards that end and, as he had expected, found that the lights were still burning in the Wichita marshal's office. What he had not expected to find was a wire waiting for him from Linton which simplified his task enormously.

Before leaving Linton, he had let it be known to his own deputies that they could contact him at the marshal's office here. Fletcher handed him the flimsy telegram which said, 'Night watchman Howard has left town Learnt that he is wanted in New York Case of robbery is suspended for lack of witness or other evidence'.

Jeremiah Hammond read the communication over several times. In spite of what he had said to his men, he could not be altogether sure that they had not engineered this; they were both fond of Esther and might have done so regardless of her father's wishes. Whatever the circumstances, he now found himself feeling profoundly grateful to them. His wish to haul an errant daughter back in disgrace had vanished away to nothing. All he hoped now was to rescue the child from the consequences of her own folly.

Fletcher, after giving him time to read the telegram, said, 'We need to talk about what happens next with the Barker case, marshal.'

'I have no official standing here, deputy. You need not address me as though I am your superior or anything of that sort.'

'Well then, we still need to talk about the business.'

'What business?' asked Hammond, a little irritably. 'The man you wanted is dead and so too are his father and one of his brothers. From all that I am able to apprehend, the affair is finished.'

'Begging your pardon, marshal, I mean Mr Hammond, that is not how I see things at all, not by a long sight. That family are as mean a bunch as you could hope to meet. All of them have been in gaol and we most likely don't know the half of what they have been up to over the years. It was a strange thing for them to do, opening fire like that as soon as you called out. Even taking into account the fact that they were drunk, I think there is more to their activities than we currently know. There are still three brothers left though, including Bob. He is a regular desperado and is suspected of involvement in robbing a train last month. He was not at the house today, but he is somewhere hereabouts and when he hears that we have wiped out half his family, I think that he will be apt to come looking for those responsible.'

'You are hinting perhaps, that since I shot his relatives, he might be gunning for me? Well, it may be so. We shall see.'

'It's not just that. I don't think that he will be holding an inquest on who pulled the trigger. He is the sort who will fly into a rage and start firing at anybody who he feels had a hand in the thing. I know Bob Barker; he is like to a mad dog.'

Marshal Hammond was not best pleased to hear this speech. He said,

'Your partner asked me to come in on that raid up at the Barker place. I did it as a favour and, now we are talking of it, I will say straight that I took all the risks while you and he cowered behind the woodpile. Now you are trying to tell me that as a result of lending you my aid there, I have incurred another duty to help you tackle the rest of the family? Is that the strength of it?'

When Hammond mentioned cowering behind the woodpile, Dave Fletcher flushed crimson like a schoolgirl. Once the other man had finished his piece, Fletcher said, 'Do you say then that you will not help?'

'No, I don't say anything of the kind. I am arguing that I have no moral obligation to do so.'

This was too high falutin' for a simple man like Fletcher, who said, 'So I can count upon you?'

'Yes. Yes you can, although my own problems come first. Where is this famous gunman at the present time?'

'I have an idea that he and his two

brothers are up in Hutchinson. Bad news travels fast and I would be surprised if somebody is not already on the way to tell him what has happened.'

'Well then,' said Hammond. 'The lightning is not liable to fall tonight. I will wager that we will not see this trouble erupt until tomorrow at the earliest. I am going home to bed now and have a deal to do on my own account early in the morning. Howsoever, if I am spared until midday, I shall come here and we will talk matters over.'

Hammond was dog-tired when he got back to Mr Chang's house — tired and feeling like he was on deadly teeter totter. One moment, everything was looking up and he thought that things might pan out, the next, disaster looming for both him and his child. Perhaps the old Chinaman read some of this in the marshal's face when he opened the door to him, because he invited Hammond to share a pot of tea with him.

If it were not sacrilegious to make the comparison, Jeremiah Hammond found that Mr Chang's back room put him in mind of a church. There was the smell of incense, the statue, the flowers and the holy book lying near at hand. If anybody had asked him two weeks ago what the eternal fate of unbaptized heathens amounted to, Hammond would have had not the least hesitation in consigning them to perdition. Now, sitting there with an old man who had heard of, and presumably rejected, the Lord Jesus, he was not so sure. He said to Chang, quite without meaning to, 'I killed two men this day.'

The Chinaman asked quietly, 'What happen? You set out to kill them or they try to kill you first?'

'Well, they had guns and they had already taken a shot at me. If I had not fired first, I would be dead now.'

'Then their evil bounced back on them. Like man who throws a stone at a wall and it comes back and hits him. Law of the world.'

'That's a mighty comforting thought to take to bed with me,' said Marshal Hammond. 'You always have the way of making a man feel better, Mr Chang. I don't know how you do it.'

The old man smiled. 'Not me. I read about the way and then tell what I find in old writings. Thank Kung Fu Tse. You hear word of your daughter?'

'Yes, I think so.'

'What now if you find her?'

'I shall take her home with me and protect her the best way I know how,' said Hammond in a low but passionate voice. 'I have made her what she is.'

'Great change of mind,' observed the old man.

'Yet I found the answer in the Bible,' said Hammond. 'The sins of the father are visited upon the children. That is what has happened in this case. My character, my sins have punished that child. I made her.'

Mr Chang smiled. 'Good to find these things before is too late, I think.'

Jeremiah Hammond smiled back.

'Yes, I think so too. I do not know what will become of me and her, but I must try to mend the harm I have done.' He stood up. 'Goodnight, Mr Chang. I hope that we shall meet again, if I am spared. But tomorrow promises to be a tricky row to hoe and no mistake.'

7

To his absolute amazement, Jeremiah Hammond woke the next morning with a good feeling about the day ahead. It was, on the face of it, quite mad. He still did not know where his daughter was to be found and even when he did track her down, there was every possibility that she would refuse his help. On top of that, at least one and possibly three or more hard men were almost certain to be on their way to settle scores with the marshal who had killed their own father and brothers. Looked at from outside, this was hardly a day to be glad on.

In spite of, or perhaps perversely because of all this, Hammond had the air of a schoolboy on the first day of the summer vacation. He felt as though he was right with the world after a good long time when he had been at odds with it. It now looked to him that, as he had told old Mr Chang last night, this was truly a case where the sins of the father had been visited upon the child. Something had happened in Esther's childhood to cause her to turn out this way and since he had had the raising of her, it was plain that he had the greater part of the responsibility for how she had become. All he could hope for now was that she would allow him to ask forgiveness and try to mend the hurt he had caused.

The marshal turned his thoughts to Bob Barker and how that situation might develop. This was a more cheerful theme, for he had in the past gone up against many violent and dangerous men, and every time he had emerged the victor. There was no reason to suppose that this day would prove any different. From what he had seen of the Barker place, they were no more than a set of drunken reprobates and he had dealt with many such.

Mr Chang greeted Marshal Hammond with a wide smile when he came down the stairs. 'I see a man at peace with himself,' said the Chinaman.

'Well, well, that is as may be. I shall not be at peace with some people before the day is out, but let come what may. I hope and pray that I shall see you later this day, Mr Chang.'

It lacked a few minutes to eight, when Marshal Hammond arrived in the vicinity of The Lucky Strike saloon in Delano. He had worked out a careful plan for examining every building around that part of the town and figuring out which might be renting out rooms. There were more than he guessed at first. Every time a cattle drive fetched up here from Texas, there would be places needed for all the cowboys who arrived with the steers. Letting rooms was quite an industry in Wichita and Delano. Apart from the hotels, boarding houses and so on, many private residences rented out accommodation on the side, as did stores. There was nothing for it, the marshal would have to knock on every likely door.

Before he set out on the wearisome task of conducting door to door enquiries, Hammond asked in the nearby stores and almost immediately found somebody who claimed to know where the young couple were staying. Frustratingly, the directions he was given did not lead to anywhere with a room to let. The woman living in the apartment though thought that she had seen somebody matching Esther's appearance, but had seen her up by the bridge.

The morning wore away in this fashion, with many people having seen, or claiming to have seen Esther and Chris Turner, but not one able to give concise and coherent directions to where they might be found. After three hours of this, Hammond recollected himself and realized that he had promised Fletcher that he would help him out in the event that any of the relatives of the men he had shot came looking for mischief. He was desperately keen to find Esther and get her safely back to Linton, but he had also made a promise and that too mattered. He had always been a man of his word and no matter which of his other beliefs might have gone into the melting pot, he aimed to stick ahold of that one.

The marshal gained the impression that Dave Fletcher and Jack Seagrove, the other deputy whom he had not yet met, were both a mite surprised to see him turn up that morning. 'What's wrong, boys?,' he said jovially. 'Thought I'd leave you in the lurch and not show up? Not a bit of it. If I say I'll do a thing, then I will do it.'

'We are right glad to see you, Marshal Hammond,' said Fletcher. 'I think that we are going to need all the help we can get.'

'Why, what's to do?'

'I will let Seagrove here explain. He knows more about it all than I do.'

'Well, sir,' said Jack Seagrove, 'six

weeks ago, Bob Barker and one or two of his brothers, along with some other men, robbed the mail train on the Union Pacific line. Up between Omaha and Fort Kearney. I don't know if you know the area?'

'I do, Deputy Seagrove,' said Hammond, 'but if there is going to be gunplay, I have a mind to tell you to skip the geography lesson and apprise me now of our present danger.'

'Just as you say, sir. Anyway, I have various informants, men who hang round saloons and pass on anything interesting that they hear. Both your name and also Bob Barker's have come up in the last few days.'

Fletcher cut in at this point, saying, 'You might say that Jack here runs our secret service branch.'

'Anyway,' said Seagrove, 'Barker seemingly saw your name in the newspaper and made out that he knew you. Said you'd shot a good friend of his, man called Tyler?'

'Yes, Patrick Tyler,' said Hammond. 'I

surely did kill him. I never knew that he was a friend of those Barkers though. This was a while back and some way from these parts.'

'Well, Barker was telling anybody who would listen about how he would not mind taking a shot at you. I didn't set much store by it; men often swear death and destruction to their enemies when they are in their cups. Nothing much comes of it when they sober up.'

'That's true,' said the marshal, 'I am suspecting that now somebody has rode off with the news that I have shot his pa and little brother and that he and his friends will be riding down here to settle the account. Is that what you would tell us?'

Jack Seagrove shrugged. 'Pretty much, yes.'

'Do we have any notion when these famous bandits are likely to be hitting town?'

'I hear that another of the Barker boys was nigh to their house yesterday when there was all that shooting. He and his brothers might be there now, they might be heading into town this minute. We don't know who will be with them either.'

'Well then,' said Hammond. 'We had best decide what we shall do.'

★   ★   ★

Esther was very much minded just to abandon Chris Turner and make her own way from Wichita. The only thing holding her back was that she was scared and lonely and needed to have somebody by her side. In all her life, she had never been alone for a longer trip than walking to school or visiting neighbours. The idea of booking a ticket on a railroad train and then getting off in Dodge City was a frightening one to her. If only Chris would liven up his ideas a bit.

As usual, the girl had stayed in the little room until about midday, but this whole caper was becoming more and more irksome to her. It had been a grand adventure at first and one in her father's eye to boot, but the novelty had worn off now. Chris Turner was amusing enough for an afternoon, but after spending days on end in his company, she was realizing what a useless clod he really was. Although she did not put it so in her own thoughts, the fact was that Turner had outlived his usefulness. He had helped her to leave Linton and enabled her to have fun in the saloons; but he was no use to her now at all, just lying on the bed brooding. She had managed to persuade him to get out in the streets with her a couple of times, but he behaved in such a suspicious manner that she was afeared that somebody would look closely at the two of them and connect them with the recent robbery.

So it was that Esther Hammond came to the point where she was ready to take her leave of Chris Turner and find somebody else to travel around with. She told Turner this at about the same time that her father was, unbeknown to her, talking earnestly with the two deputies. To her dismay and disgust, the boy began to cry. 'Esther, don't leave me. I am scared of what we done.'

'For the Lord's sake, hush up,' she said urgently. 'Somebody will be hearing you directly and then where will we be?'

'I can't help it,' he sobbed, 'I want to go home. I did not want to do any of this. You put me up to it, Esther, you know you did.'

'Well, what of it?' said the girl brusquely. 'You are the same age as me. We are both seventeen, it is not like you are a little boy who I dragged away from his mother. Although you surely do act like such sometimes.'

She was irritated and a little scared herself and this made Esther speak more roughly than might otherwise have been the case. She softened somewhat and said, 'Listen now, if you buck up, then maybe we needn't part.

Put on your boots and we will go for a walk into Wichita itself. We could have a drink in a saloon, you know. That would brace you up a little.'

'I don't know,' said Chris, 'I would rather stay here for a spell.'

'Then before God, you can stay here alone,' said Esther angrily. 'I mean it, Chris. Either you come out with me right this very minute or we part company for good and all.'

Under such a threat, Chris Turner washed, shaved and made himself presentable. Then the two of them walked along the river to the bridge and crossed over into Wichita.

Marshal Hammond and the two deputies were getting themselves ready for what looked to be a trying and dangerous encounter. There was little point in participating in a gunfight without the necessary weapons and so Fletcher had opened up the armoury: a walk in closet where a store of shotguns, rifles and various large calibre pistols were kept, along with boxes of ammunition.

Jack Seagrove had noticed that Hammond was equipped only with his old Colt Dragoon. 'Pardon me for saying so, Marshal Hammond, but you are not proposing to take part in what might be a lively contest armed only with an old cap and ball pistol like that?'

'It has stood me in good stead, these many years,' replied Hammond coldly. His own deputies had been urging him for years to carry something a little more up-to-date and modern. 'Those double action handguns don't suit me,' he told Seagrove. 'You pull that hard on the trigger to raise up the hammer, that it compromises your aim. This little beauty, why, once it is cocked, I could fire it by no more than blowing on the trigger.'

'We have not the least idea how many men will be coming with Barker,' Seagrove reminded him. 'I suppose you keep an empty chamber under the hammer? That gives you just five shots before you reload. You are surely not going to be fooling around with a flask of powder and a ramrod, not in the middle of a gun battle.'

It was a familiar enough debate, but for once, Hammond decided that there was some merit in the argument. If he was up against only one or two men, then he would seldom want more than five shots. But suppose that Bob Barker turned up in Wichita with a whole posse of roughnecks, what then?

So it was that the marshal had agreed to browse through the weaponry which was contained in the 'armoury'. If there really was the chance of a big shoot-out, then he would allow that there might be good reason to carry something extra. He took down a Winchester 73 from the rack and worked the lever a few times. The action seemed smooth enough and so he took that and also a standard .45 which used brass cartridges, rather than the powder and caps that he was used to. He took a couple of boxes of shells as well.

Fletcher and Seagrove just took rifles. Their policy was simple. If any bad men were going to be coming their way with the avowed intention of causing mayhem, then the deputies wanted to be able to stop those men dead at a couple of hundred yards distance, not stand right up close and trade bullets from revolvers.

There had been some slight discussion between Hammond and the other two as to the advisability of riding out to meet the trouble outside the town limits. Nobody wanted shooting on the streets of Wichita. Set against this was the fact that they did not know for sure from which direction the Barkers and their associates would be coming. It was most likely, of course, that they would have stopped off at the farmhouse, if only to lay out the corpses of their near family members. Under normal circumstances, the marshal's office would have arranged for an undertaker to deal with the men who had been killed, but with the threat of violence hanging in the air, it would not have been right to send civilians into hazard in that way.

The three of them finally agreed that they should stay together and just ride patrol around the approaches to Wichita. It would of course be far better if any armed confrontation did not take place on the very streets of the town, but nothing could be guaranteed.

Seagrove had spoken to one of his informants, who had told him that the Barkers would be entering the town from the north. Even assuming that they were a little cunning and skirted around a bit before heading into Wichita, this would at most mean that they might come in from the east or west. They would hardly travel all the way round in order to approach from the south. Seagrove therefore suggested, and Fletcher agreed, that they should limit their patrol to the north and a short way to the east and west. The experience that Marshal Hammond had had of paid informants led him to be distinctly dubious about this scheme. He voiced his doubts, but since the other two were in favour and he did not in any case have any sort of official standing in the town, he went along with what the other two suggested, although not without serious misgivings.

Hammond flatly refused to have the same horse as he had drawn on the raid the previous day. Fletcher joshed him a little, saying, 'Why, that is right ungrateful of you. That beast saved your life yesterday by skittering out of the way when old man Barker opened up on you!'

'Yes,' said Hammond grimly, 'and another time, it is likely enough to take me the wrong way and carry me into the path of a bullet. No, I want a quiet and reliable horse, thank you all the same.'

The three lawmen mounted up and rode in silence to the edge of town, where the buildings of Wichita gave way to the patchwork of fields which stretched out into the distance. Then they began circling the town at a leisurely trot.

* * *

Once he was out on the streets and in the fresh air, Turner did feel a bit better. Esther had been right about that. There did not appear to be as many folk about as usual. Although they did not know it, Fletcher and Seagrove had been spreading the word that unless folk had strong reason to be out and about, this might be a good day for staying indoors at home. Not everybody had taken the advice, but a significant enough proportion to make the streets noticeably less crowded than usual.

* * *

As they trotted around the roads on the edge of town, the marshal and two deputies talked in a desultory way about this and that, the conversation chiefly concerning itself with shootouts in which they had been caught up. Actually, regular firefights with groups of men exchanging shots were far from a common occurrence. Most of the action that they had all seen was just one man taking shots at them, while they returned fire. The incident in which Hammond and Fletcher had been mixed up the day before was sufficiently out of the ordinary for Seagrove to regret not having been a part of it.

'I mind, Mr Hammond,' said Seagrove, 'that being so much older than us, you must have seen more gun battles like the one yesterday?'

'I have seen one or two,' admitted the marshal. 'But few that ended in such a bloody conclusion. When it comes right down to it, few men are really careless of their lives and most will not push things to the point of death.'

'Well, those Barkers surely did that,' said Dave Fletcher.

'They were in drink,' said Hammond. 'That room they were in fairly reeked of poteen. That stuff makes men act crazy. Without that encouragement, I don't think that we would have had such a bad ending.'

Seagrove said, 'So you think that today will just fizzle out into nothing — if, that is, there is no drink involved?'

'I would not be surprised,' said Marshal Hammond. 'It is certainly my devout hope. I do not wish to kill anybody.'

★   ★   ★

Esther Hammond had not been altogether open and honest with Chris. Although she truly was sick of him lying in that room moping, she wanted him to come out and about with her for a purpose. She was developing quite a taste for alcohol and very much wanted to have a few drinks of whiskey. Although she had not got herself into the state that Chris had, she had still found the business of the man they attacked getting so badly hurt a little alarming. After a few glasses of liquor though, she did not worry about a thing and had the feeling that nothing could harm her. It had been a few days last since she had experienced that feeling of invincibility and she lacked the confidence to enter a saloon alone. Her scheme in getting Chris up and about tended towards persuading him into taking her to a saloon so that she could get a little tipsy.

'Hey, Chris,' said the girl, as they neared the centre of Wichita. 'What say we have a little drink to cheer us up? You have been right down in the dumps lately and it might set the spring back in your walk.'

'I don't know, Esther,' he said. 'I don't want you to start drawing attention to us like you have done in the past. It would not answer in our present situation.'

'Landsakes, Chris, I am talking about a glass or two of whiskey, that's all.

Don't be such an old woman.'

'Well,' said Turner, wavering. 'I suppose it would do no harm. And I could do with loosening up a little. Perhaps you are right, I need to relax myself.'

'That's the boy!' said Esther. 'Come on, this place looks as good as any.'

★　★　★

Marshal Hammond reined in his horse on a rise of ground which commanded a good view of the area to the north of the town. 'Hutchinson is over in yonder direction, is that right?' he asked.

'Yes,' said Seagrove, 'and the Barker place is over there, to the right. Why, of course you know. I was forgetting that you went there with Pete and Dave here.'

'What's to hinder those boys from coming down the road there as though passing your town and then doubling back and coming up from behind us?'

'You worry too much, begging your

159

pardon,' said Seagrove. 'Those fellows are not that crafty. They do not even know we are on to them. Trust me, we will see them coming and have time to stop them at a distance.'

One thing which Jeremiah Hammond took as an article of faith only slightly less certain-sure than Scripture, was that when a man told you to trust him, then that was the very last thing you ought to do. He looked around uneasily and in his own mind at least, the thing was quite settled: any danger would be coming from the south.

★ ★ ★

After they had had two glasses of rye whiskey apiece, Chris Turner began to think that Esther was right and that he worried too much. As for Esther herself, she was a different person when drinking. Fond of her as he was, he could not deny that she had a shrewish streak which had come to the fore in the last couple of days. Now she was drinking, all that had vanished.

'What do you say to trying some-where else?' said Esther. 'This place is not what I would call lively.'

'It is not far past noon,' Turner replied. 'I guess most folks is working and cannot spend time in saloons.'

'More fool them!' said Esther. They wandered from the saloon in search of somewhere with a better atmosphere. They didn't know it, but their search was leading them towards the marshal's office, which was currently closed up.

* * *

Not least of the sound reasons that Marshal Hammond had for distrusting informants was the tendency which he had often noted in such people to hunt with the hounds and run with the fox. In short, just because you were paying them, this did not mean at all that they were not getting money from other sources at the same time. He was right to be suspicious of

Seagrove's informant, because this man, although he had been paid well by the deputy, was also in touch with Bob Barker and had sent him a message, advising him that if he was making a visit to Wichita, then he would be well advised to approach the town from the south.

So it was that while Hammond and the two deputies were scanning the horizon in the direction of Hutchinson, Bob Barker, his two brothers Jethro and Mike, together with another fellow, all rode in along the Omaha City road.

Bob Barker was not commonly given to making close friends. One of the few men he had taken a real liking to since he was a boy had been Pat Tyler. The two of them had been pretty well inseparable, drinking together, going out whoring and undertaking a variety of robberies side by side across Kansas. One day, Tyler had held up a traveller outside the town of Linton and found himself being ruthlessly pursued by the marshal there. This dedicated individual had tracked Patrick Tyler for miles and then when he caught up with him and Tyler was inclined to offer resistance, he had shot him down in the road like a dog. Barker had marked the name of the man who had done this deed and it was on his list of those with whom he would one day have a reckoning.

You could say any number of harsh things about old man Barker and his sons. They were shiftless, troublesome, dishonest, violent and often operating on the wrong side of the law. One thing which nobody could deny was that they loved each other. The old man loved his boys, they loved him and all the brothers were tolerable fond of each other as well. When Bob Barker had received word of what had happened at his father's house, he rode at a furious speed from Hutchinson and when he entered that house and found the corpses of his father and two of his brothers, he wept like a baby. When he had finished, he dried his eyes and swore bloody vengeance on the man who had killed his father, two of his brothers and best friend.

8

There was no sign of anybody at the marshal's office and so Bob Barker drew his pistol and shot out the windows. His brother Mike did the same with the windows of a few neighbouring properties. Passers-by began to flee in alarm and within a minute or two at most, the street near the office was deserted. The four men sat on their horses and waited for Hammond, and also anybody else who felt like thwarting their wishes, to come and get what was waiting for them.

Marshal Hammond and the two deputies heard the shooting coming from the centre of town and knew at once that they had been misled. Hammond did not bother even to hint at such childish sentiments as, 'I told you so'. He just said, 'I think there is need of us,' and turned his horse's head south.

Now the response of most ordinary, sane and level-headed persons to the sound of gunfire is to flee precipitately away from it. Lawmen are a special case and Jeremiah Hammond and the two deputies from Wichita would have been neglecting their duty were they not to have set off at a gallop towards the shooting, which they could hear coming from the centre of town. Unfortunately, there will always be a few foolhardy and injudicious types who, on hearing shooting, will make their way to where the action is — notwithstanding the fact that whatever is taking place is no affair of theirs. Esther Hammond and Chris Turner were drinking in a tavern just down the road aways from the marshal's office and when they heard the shots, as Bob Barker and his relatives and friend began to shoot the place up, Esther said at once, 'Hey, it sounds like something interesting is happening. Let's go take a look, Chris.'

The few other patrons in the Poor Struggler at that time of day, had more sense than the youngsters. At the first sign of trouble, they had thrown themselves to the sawdust covered floor and were not intending even to look from the windows, lest they intercepted a bullet in some vital part of their anatomy. Chris Turner was disposed to join these folk on the floor, because he had no curiosity about the gunfire and did not wish to become involved.

'I don't think we should go outside, Esther,' he told her. 'Look at all these fellows here, even the barkeep. They are not rushing out into the street. They are keeping their heads down.'

The girl's eyes were glittering with a combination of whiskey and excitement and she was not apt to be deflected from her purpose by such, as she saw it, mealy-mouthed and cowardly counsel. Although they had been having a pleasant enough time in the saloon, of a sudden she turned on her friend, saying, 'You know, I wonder sometimes what I ever saw in you, Chris Turner. If you were any sort of man, you would come with me so that we could see what is going on. It sounds right exciting.'

Greatly against his better judgement, Turner agreed to go down the street a short distance with her and just peep around the corner to see what was happening.

★　★　★

Wichita was not, in 1879, a large city and it did not take Hammond, Fletcher and Seagrove long to ride from the outskirts of town to the vicinity of their office, which was located near to the centre. As they turned the corner, they could see the whole length of the street and it was immediately apparent that the place was nigh on deserted, save for four men on horseback who were loitering a few hundred yards down the road. Right about where the office was, in fact.

The three men, Marshal Hammond and the two deputies accompanying him, had not yet been seen and so they retreated back round the corner to discuss the best course of action. The young men looked to Jeremiah Hammond for advice and he said, 'As I read it, we have two choices. We could take it as certain that those men down the street mean mischief and just sight our rifles and start shooting from here. Or, we could go up to them, ask them what they are about and challenge them to throw down their weapons. It is up to you two. I will go along with what you want to do.'

'I don't like the idea,' said Fletcher slowly, 'of shooting a man without first offering him a chance to surrender.'

Seagrove nodded his head in agreement. 'It would be a scurvy trick to play, even upon villains like that.'

'I am of the same mind,' said Hammond. 'It would go against the grain for me to shoot any man unawares. Howsoever, if we ride down that street now towards them, they will have time to identify us all and I do not know if they share our code of honour. They might just kill us before we came within hailing distance of them.'

'What then?' said Fletcher.

'Why don't we leave our horses here and then move stealthily round the back of the stores, until we are practically on top of them? Then we could cock our pieces, take aim and call upon them from cover. It would still give them a chance to give up, but might tilt the odds somewhat in our favour.'

The scheme that Hammond put forward found favour in the eyes of the deputies. They tethered their horses to a rail and made off round the alleyways behind the saloons and stores which ran along the street.

'Nothing is happening,' said Esther Hammond, sounding disappointed. 'We should have come straight out, instead of dithering about.' The two youngsters were looking round a storefront at the four mounted men outside the marshal's office. There were some grounds for feeling, as the girl evidently did, that nothing was happening. The four riders sat at their ease, smoking and idling, like they did not have a care in the world. Had it not been for the shooting earlier, anybody watching them now might think that they were merely killing time before going off on a picnic or something similar.

Appearances are all too often deceptive, and Bob Barker and his three accomplices were in reality anything at all but relaxed. It was part of their habitual façade though, for none of them ever to appear outwardly concerned about anything much. But for all that they looked to be chatting among themselves in a carefree and inconsequential fashion, all four were keyed up and prepared either to do murder or be killed in their turn.

Esther Hammond could not, of course, at the age of seventeen, be reasonably expected to know any of this. To her, the fun and games had ended and all she saw were a bunch of amiable looking fellows sitting on their horses and talking together as though there was nothing amiss. She did not even realize that these were the men who had been responsible for shooting up the nearby store fronts. She was almost on the point of going right up to the men and asking them what had been going on. Indeed, she had shaken off Chris Turner's restraining hand and taken the first step into the open street when she gave a gasp of horror. There, on the other side of the street, was her father.

Her father did not look as though he had seen her and so Esther shrank back into the shadows. She and Turner were in a narrow little lane which led off the main street. From what she had seen, her father and two other men were hiding in another such lane between buildings and they had been, like her, peering cautiously at the four riders. Esther was torn between a desire to run away at once and so avoid her father's wrath and the overwhelming desire to watch what would next chance. The whiskey that she had been drinking over the last hour clouded her faculties to the extent that she made the wrong decision at this point and chose to remain where she was and see the show.

Hammond and the other two men had moved swiftly but silently along the back of the stores, until they were close to the office. Then they found a gap between buildings and so reached the street. 'I reckon we had best prepare ourselves for action,' said the marshal, matching the deed to the words by cocking the Winchester. Fletcher and Seagrove did the same with their own rifles. 'Who wants to make the call?' enquired Hammond.

'You can, if you will,' said Dave Fletcher.

With no hesitation or further debate, Jeremiah Hammond leaned round the corner of the building, drew down on the nearest of the men that he could see and cried in a loud voice, 'Throw down your weapons. You are surrounded and if you make any other move, we will shoot.'

The words were scarcely out of his mouth, before a withering fire was directed at him. He fired once before withdrawing into the shelter of the alleyway and had the satisfaction of seeing the man he had been aiming at fall from his horse.

'They are damned quick off the mark,' said Seagrove. 'I mind that there is little intention there to throw down their weapons.'

'You might well draw that conclusion,' said Hammond dryly. When the fire from the opposing party slackened somewhat, he leaned out, snapped off another couple of shots and then retreated again. His brief look was enough to assure him that the man he had shot had not risen from the ground and was certainly out of the game. 'One down and three to go,' he remarked.

When the fresh bout of shooting

began, Esther at first put her hands over her ears like a little girl. Then, feeling that she had shamed herself by doing so, she tried to affect a nonchalance that she was very far from feeling. In spite of all that she had said about hating her father, she knew that those men in the road were trying to kill him in earnest and the thought scared her. However much he had irked her over the years of her childhood, she did not wish him dead.

Hammond said to Fletcher and Seagrove, 'Well boys, we can't let this go on all day. It will cast into hazard the decent, law-abiding citizens who are cowering in their homes. Somebody will be getting killed by a stray shot if we stay cowering here much longer.' The two deputies looked at him enquiringly, eager to hear his suggestion. He continued, 'I am going to run to that store over the way there. While those fellows are firing at me, you two mark them well and see if you can catch them unawares. When I am safely there, they will be forced to divide their fire between us and this should give us an edge. After all, they are in the open and we are not. Also, we are using rifles and they seem only to have pistols.'

The men outside the marshal's office were not firing now. They were evidently waiting to see what would next happen. None of them expected to see Jeremiah Hammond sprinting from one side of the street to the other and they hesitated for a fraction of a second. Then the deputies from Wichita opened up on them and they had to take their eyes from Hammond in order to return fire.

As soon as he was in the store, the owner of which was crouched behind his counter in fear, Hammond crawled to the window and smashed it with the butt of his rifle. The breaking glass attracted a hail of fire from the street. The marshal waited until it died down before looking from the window. Meanwhile, Fletcher and Seagrove kept popping their heads round the corner of the building and engaging their opponents. This kept the three men on horseback fully occupied and, as he had expected, they momentarily forgot all about the marshal. He stood up and fired two carefully aimed shots, bringing down another of the men. Before the two survivors had a chance to reply, he ducked back out of sight. The set-up was a neat one now and with a little good fortune, he and the other two would be able to fire from cover like this with their rifles until they had killed the other men as well.

To Marshal Hammond's horror, he saw Dave Fletcher now bolt from the alley-way, coming towards him. Neither then nor later was he ever able to figure out what the young man had been about when he made this move. After he had himself run across the road like that, the men shooting at them would be alert to such a gambit being tried again. So it proved, because half way across the street, a bullet caught the deputy and he stumbled and fell.

Hammond immediately tried to draw their fire, by losing off a couple of shots at them, but it was too late. As soon as Fletcher was down, both the remaining gunmen fired at him as he lay there. As they concentrated their attention on the fallen man, Hammond was able to pick off another of them. Only one was now left.

'Are you ready to surrender now?' called the marshal, 'Or will you go the same way as your partners?'

The single survivor of the four men who had started the shooting had moved out of sight. He shouted back, 'Well now, that depends. Is that man we killed Jeremiah Hammond?'

'No, you cowson,' called back Hammond, resorting for once to vulgarity. 'He is alive and well here and will soon put half an ounce of lead through your heart.'

Now there was no way that Bob Barker, who was the only man left alive on the outlaw side of the shootout, could know how many men were concealed out of his sight. He probably guessed that even if he lit out right this minute without further ado, he would have a posse hot on his heels which would bring him back for trial and eventual hanging. That at any rate was how Hammond later figured the man's actions, because instead of either showing defiance by firing at them again or simply turning tail and running, Barker took it into his head to seize a hostage.

Esther had been growing more and more thrilled by events as the gun battle raged. For one thing, she had never in her life heard guns being fired in anger and for another this was her own father taking down a set of villains. There was something kind of impressive about it, or so she thought. Chris Turner was in a different state entirely. He was terrified out of his wits and kept clutching at the girl's sleeve to draw her back. He feared, with some justification, that she would end up with a bullet through her head if she carried on exposing herself in this way. When Bob Barker spurred on his horse straight towards them, the boy and girl reacted in very different ways. Esther just stood there, unable to work out what was happening, while Chris Turner grabbed her arm to try and hustle her away to safety.

Barker said urgently, 'You girl, you stand to. I want you up here with me, for we are going on a little ride together.'

Turner said, 'Leave her be. She is nothing to do with this.' He tried to move in front of Esther to shield her from the man waving a pistol at them.

'I will not ask twice,' said Barker. 'You boy, move away from her now.' When there was no sign that Chris Turner was intending to comply with this instruction, Bob Barker shot him dead on the spot. Esther began screaming hysterically.

By this time, Marshal Hammond could tell that the fighting was over and that the surviving member of the gang was about to make his getaway. He emerged from the store with his rifle cocked and ready. Deputy Seagrove came out of the alley where he had been sheltering at the same time and the two of them began walking past the slain body of their comrade towards where they supposed that the last of the men would be found, although he was not presently in view. When the screaming began, Hammond knew at once that it was his daughter's voice and he broke into a run.

Having killed Turner, Bob Barker reached down and grabbed hold of Esther's wrist. 'Come on, little lady,' he said. 'Up you come.' He hauled the terrified girl up, to sit before him. Her skirt rucked up and even in the middle of the deadliest of danger, she was still embarrassed and did her best to cover herself. Barker said, 'No matter about showing your petticoats and drawers.'

Having somehow succeeding in getting the girl seated in front of him on the saddle, Barker emerged from the alleyway to find the marshal and deputy about forty or fifty feet from him. He put his pistol to the girl's head and said, 'Either one of you makes me nervous and I am going to kill this girl. Same goes if I am pursued or shot at. I will make sure to live long enough to pull the trigger and finish her.'

Esther Hammond caught sight of her father and screamed out, 'Daddy!'

'Daddy?' said Barker in amazement. 'Why I call this as good as a play. That was a lucky chance, finding a lawman's daughter by the side of the road. Remember now, any trouble and she dies first.' Then he wheeled round and set off at a sedate trot, confident that the girl's father would not molest him in any way.

It would have been mad folly to chase right after the man who had captured his child. This much, Hammond knew instinctively. He said to Seagrove, 'Do you know which of them that was?'

'Yes,' was the reply. 'That was the famous Bob Barker himself.'

'Tell me,' asked Marshal Hammond. 'Would you say that he is a man who threatens and bluffs, or is he rather one of those who carries out what he says he will do?'

The deputy did not hesitate. He said, 'Listen now, if Bob Barker says he'll do a thing, then it is as good as done. He is not boastful and nor does he brag, but just tells things as they are. He said he would shoot that girl if he was pursued and I believe that that is just exactly what he will do.'

Hammond felt two conflicting emotions, each tugging him in the opposite direction from the other. On the one hand, he felt great satisfaction that Chris Turner was now dead and that the only thing linking his daughter to the killing of Grover McPherson was out of the reckoning for good. On the other hand, he felt terror at the fact that the child was now in the hands of a ruthless outlaw. Neither of these feelings had any reference to Scripture or religion, which was strange considering the type of man that Hammond was. They were deep and visceral urges and fears such as any father might fall prey to. Whatever else befell him on this trip, Jeremiah Hammond knew that something had changed within him and that things would never be the same again in his life.

His immediate urge was to ride straight off in pursuit of his daughter. Still and all, he felt that he should at least first lend a hand clearing up the aftermath of the gunplay.

The first melancholy task which Hammond and Seagrove undertook was to carry the body of Dave Fletcher into a store and set it gently on a table there. Having done this, they went to sort through the carnage in the street outside the marshal's office. One of the horses ridden by the men was dead and another was lying in the road, unable to get up and whinnying pitifully. Seagrove dispatched it with a bullet through the ear. What became of the third riderless horse, nobody ever knew. It had run off during the shooting and was never seen again.

There were four corpses to deal with, apart of course from Fletcher's. Hammond and Seagrove dragged them onto the sidewalk and laid them side by side. Seagrove said, 'These two are Barker boys. This here is Jethro and that is Michael. I don't know who these other two are.'

'Well I recognize one of them. This boy is called Chris Turner.'

'How do you come to know him? He looks awful young to be riding with outlaws.'

'He wasn't with these fellows. I guess he was just in the street,' said Marshal Hammond, neatly evading any explanation of how he came to know the boy.

Now that everything had calmed down, the citizens of Wichita were drifting onto the scene to tut and say things like, 'Lordy, what a to do!' and 'My, fancy such a thing happening here, of all places.' They viewed the four corpses as though they were a waxwork exhibition, until Marshal Hammond, feeling a mite disgusted, reproved them by saying, 'Show some respect for these men, now. They are dead. This is not a carnival sideshow.'

Once the undertaker had been sent for and folk reassured that no more trouble was on the horizon, Seagrove opened up the office and brewed up some coffee for him and Hammond.

'What is your purpose now?' asked Seagrove.

'Why, to ride after him you call Bob Barker and free my daughter, of course.'

'You don't look to be in a hurry.'

'It would be madness to let him see me today. He would shoot the girl in front of me. He owes me an injury in any case and so might kill my daughter whether or not I pursue him. Would you think him capable of such viciousness?'

'I would not have said so, no,' said Seagrove, trying to be fair to Barker. 'He will shoot any man, even for looking at him in the wrong way, but I don't think he would kill a girl like that just for meanness.'

'Could I appeal to his honour? Would he face me in a fair fight? Meaning just the two of us, man to man?'

'He might do at that, but I would not bet on it.'

Hammond stood up and walked around the office. He said, 'Would you let me borrow that horse I rode today?'

'Buster? Sure, keep him as long as you have need.'

'Where do you think Barker will be heading?'

'North. He won't hole up at his father's house, nor Hutchinson either. I mind I told you that he was suspected of holding up a mail train on the Union Pacific? At a guess, I would say that he has friends up that way, maybe even what one might term a gang.'

'The road forks after leaving here to the north, doesn't it? One way goes to Topeka and the other to Lincoln and Fort Kerney. Which path will he take?'

'Fort Kerney,' said Seagrove promptly. 'It was just outside there that the train was ambushed.'

Hammond walked slowly down the street to where he had left Buster tethered up. It was not a marvellous specimen as far as horses went, but then he was not aiming to enter it in a race or dressage show. It would be enough if the creature would just bear him safely for forty miles or so. It looked as though it would be tough enough for a little adventuring off the beaten track and that mattered far more than breeding or looks.

9

If Jeremiah Hammond knew anything about men like Bob Barker, then he guessed that for the first half hour or so, the man would be turning in the saddle every thirty seconds, in order to peer back for signs of a posse coming after him. Once he was clear, then he would relax a bit. At this point, one of two things would happen. He would either abandon the girl so that he could make better speed or he would hang onto her for a day or so and hope to use her as a bargaining counter if apprehended. There was a third option, but it was one that Hammond could not bear to consider. This was that Barker would kill Esther out of spite. True, Seagrove thought it unlikely that he would behave in this way, but there was no real accounting for the ways of wicked men.

Before saddling up and leaving Wichita, Marshal Hammond bought a few basic provisions, including a warm blanket. It was not the weather to be sleeping out in the open, but it might yet come to that pass. He called in at the office to bid Jack Seagrove farewell.

'I do not think that I will be gone that long,' Hammond said to the deputy. 'With good fortune and the will of God, I might catch up with him by nightfall.'

It was a little after three in the afternoon by the time that Jeremiah Hammond left the town. He purposed to ride along the road that he thought Barker would be taking and to keep a sharp eye out for the man. If he saw him, Hammond intended to ride cross country and so outflank him. Barker's horse was carrying two people, which would tend to make for slow travelling. If the marshal kept a fairly lively pace, then he could well overtake the man who was holding his daughter before nightfall.

As he rode, Hammond considered the events of the last week. He had come to realize that for all his talk of raising up a child in the way he should go, that he did not really know his daughter at all. His sister Caroline had hinted that the girl was not as God-fearing as he had believed, but what this might mean in practice he had not the least notion. It had been enough for him that Esther's outward behaviour had been respectable and correct. He had given little thought to what she was like within — which, thought Hammond, just about sums up how I have been working for most of my life, judging by appearances. The godly go to church and the wicked hang round bar-rooms. He knew of course, deep inside, that often it was the other way round and you found wicked men in the house of God and devout ones in a tavern. After all, didn't our Lord himself consort with publicans and sinners? Nevertheless, he had got into the way of taking these things at face value.

* * *

The effects of the whiskey that she had drunk earlier had altogether worn off and there was no bravado about Esther Hammond now. She was a thoroughly scared young girl who wanted her father to take care of her. Almost all her life, she had been trying to free herself of his interference and control; now, she would have welcomed it. However harsh he might be with her, she just wished that she could be back in her bedroom, with Aunt Caroline and her father sitting downstairs. As she thought of this, tears began to prick her eyes and she gave a muffled sob.

'Hey,' said Bob Barker, 'What are you about? Crying, is it? There is no need. I am not about to harm you. Don't set mind to what I said back there about shooting you. I have never harmed a female in the whole course of my life. I ain't about to start now.'

'Where are you taking me?'

'I ain't exactly taking you anywhere in particular. I cannot just set you down here in the middle of nowhere. When we get to Abilene, I will let you go. In the meantime, do not be afeared. No harm will come to you.'

They were proceeding at a trot and it was a pleasant enough evening, although a little chilly. Esther said, 'How far is it to Abilene?'

'Some miles. We shall not reach it this day. Tell me now, is your father that Bible thumping lawman from Linton?'

The girl smiled at this succinct description. 'He is Jeremiah Hammond, if that is what you mean.'

'Well, I have a crow to pluck with him and that is a fact. He killed a good friend of mine some time since and in the past few days has massacred my entire family. I never knew one man who has caused me more harm.'

Marshal Hammond rode on, sometimes at a trot and then at other times cantering along at a brisk pace. He could see no sign of his quarry ahead of him and kept a sharp eye on any cover on either side of the road. He did not aim to fall victim to an ambush. And still, his mind wrestled with the question of his daughter and the extent to which he was to blame for how she had turned out. If it was true that she had turned out bad — and from all that he had been able to collect in recent days, nothing was more likely — then he would have to help her get straight again; how that was to be done, the good Lord alone knew.

By the time that twilight arrived, Hammond had still not caught up with Barker and his daughter. He slowed right down and let Buster proceed at a walk. Whatever else did or did not happen in the future with his child, the one thing he surely had to tell her was that he had a measure of guilt for how things had happened. He had often enough condemned some mother or father for the way that their offspring turned out and he was not a big enough hypocrite now to reject that same line of reasoning for his own family. The sins of the fathers had been visited upon the children and if Esther Hammond was really a thief and a killer, then the responsibility for those crimes could be laid just as much at his own door as they could be blamed on Esther.

* * *

'I do not aim to be riding in the dark,' Bob Barker told the girl that he had seized. 'It would be a bad business for the both of us if this beast were to break a leg or something of that sort.'

The girl craned her head around and looked in every direction. 'I see no lights,' she observed. 'Where are we to stay? Is there a town nearby?'

'No, and even were there to be, I would not be planning on staying in it.

There is an old place that me and my boys use, it is just off the road aways. We will have to get down and lead the horse a little.'

Barker dismounted and then helped down the girl. He said, 'You are not about to run off or scream or anything, I suppose?'

'No,' said Esther. 'It is powerful dark and I would not know where to go.'

'I was thinking more on your own interest, anyway,' said Barker. 'Having dragged you out here, I feel kind of responsible for you.'

The two of them walked up a grassy slope in companionable silence. Esther was not the least bit scared, which she found strange. This man was, after all, a cold-blooded killer. The Lord knew what his future plans might entail. At length, they came to a ruined stone building, little more than two standing walls of which remained. 'There's no roof!' exclaimed Esther, 'What sort of shelter do you call this?'

'I call it the only sort of shelter we

will have this night.'

Bob Barker secured the horse to a nearby tree and then came back with the saddle-bag. 'Are you hungry?' he asked.

'I am very hungry.'

'Well, there is only bread, cheese and cold meat. We can wash it down with water from yonder stream. I will fill the canteens.'

When he returned, Barker said to the girl, 'You look cold.' He ferreted around and produced a thick army blanket. 'Here, wrap this around yourself. You will need it to keep out the chill at night, in any case.'

'Won't you be cold, though?' asked Esther.

'That's nothing to the purpose. I have slept out without a blanket before and in colder weather than this.'

★ ★ ★

An hour after the sun had slipped below the horizon, Jeremiah Hammond was quite sure that he would have overtaken the man who had his daughter. He reined in and considered the matter. Either this was the wrong road and Barker had been bound for Lincoln after all, or he had left this road to rest up for the night. Marshal Hammond turned these possibilities over in his mind. Then it came to him that a desperado like this must have little boltholes scattered here and there. He hated the idea of his daughter being compelled to spend the night with such a man as this, but what can't be cured, must be endured and he gave this aspect of the thing no further thought.

Thinking of the man as a 'desperado' set Hammond on the right path and he knew at once just precisely where Barker was going. It would mean riding through the night, but that was nothing, as long as he did not push his horse too hard. As long as they took regular breaks, it should be possible to get ahead of Barker and meet him on Jeremiah Hammond's own terms. And then, by God, there would be a reckoning.

* * *

'I'm afraid that we cannot light a fire,' Barker told the girl, 'I do not know who is pursuing me and I am loathe to give them any help in running me to earth.'

'That's fine, thank you,' said Esther. 'I am warm enough in this blanket.'

'Him that I shot, was he your sweetheart or beau or something of the sort?'

'Yes, kind of, I guess.' Esther realized with a shock that she had not even thought of Chris since he had been gunned down by this man.

'I'm sorry I shot him and I can say no more than that. I had need and the thing is done. Still and all, I am sorry about it.'

'Have you killed many men?'

'That is a strange question. You are a cool one. I have never known the like! Yes, I have killed enough men in my time. I never yet harmed a woman or child though, so you need not fret about that.'

It was strange, but Esther believed this villain. In a curious way, she felt safe with him, safer than she would with many a more respectable person. True, he had grabbed her to stop anybody shooting at or arresting him, but she knew without his telling her so that he would no more think of harming her than he would of flying to the moon.

'What were you and your pa doing in Wichita, anyway?' asked Barker.

'We did not go there together. I went there and he came to fetch me back home.'

'Oh, that's the way of it, is it? You have run away from your home. Was he awful strict with you? Them religious type often are.'

The girl thought about this for a moment and then said, 'No, I could not say that he was terrible strict. He never beat me or anything. It was more that he did not seem to like folk having fun. Everything that I wanted to do was sinful. By which, I mean dancing, reading novels, walking for pleasure and talking with boys.'

The man threw back his head and laughed. 'And so you lit out and he came after you. You should be glad that he cares that much. I wanted to kill your father, I still do, but I would not say that he sounds like he has mistreated you too dreadful.'

'Did you love your own father?'

'I may as well tell you now, your father killed my own pa less than a week since. Yes, I loved him. He raised all five of us by his own self. I have lost all my family now and your pa is answerable for it. What affair of his was it to come here and start shooting my brothers so?' Barker jumped up and walked off a little way. He stood there just staring into the night and it came into Esther's mind that he was crying.

She shrugged off the blanket, got up

and went over to him. Taking his arm, she said, 'I'm sorry for your loss.'

Bob Barker turned to her and said: 'You are a right kind person. Your father might be a devil, begging your pardon, but you are kind.'

They went back and sat down once more. Why she did so, she had no idea, but Esther Hammond began to tell the outlaw about what had chanced to bring her to this pass. He listened silently, without once interrupting. She even told him about the murder of Grover McPherson. When she had finished speaking, Barker said, 'That's the hell of a tale, if you will forgive the expression. How much of this is known to others?'

'Since Chris was killed? Nobody, I guess.'

'Then if you will take my advice, you will keep it that way. Do not be tempted to unburden yourself to anybody else. The law has a long memory.'

'I thought that you might know what it was like to have done such things.'

'As to that,' said Bob Barker, his voice tinged with bitterness, 'yes, I understand what it is like. I have done worse than you and started younger, too. But it is not the same for boys. We begin by pulling the wings of flies and then progress naturally sometimes to mayhem and murder of other men. It is not to be thought of that a girl would carry on so. I am honoured by your confidence, but keep quiet about this and for the love of God, do not get mixed up in such tricks again.'

'I am sorry for what I did.'

'Yes, I am sure of it. But try to be a good girl for the future. I know where this road leads one and you would not wish to end up a hardened wretch like me, now would you?' He reached over and patted Esther's arm. 'Let us try to get to sleep now, and in the morning I will take you to a town where you may wire to your family or someone to come and fetch you.'

*   *   *

203

As he and Buster trudged north along the road, Marshal Hammond resolved that when once he had his daughter safe back home again, there would be changes made in the domestic arrangements. He minded that his sister had her own thoughts on this subject and it might be no bad thing to let her have more say in the matter. What did he know of young girls, their hopes and dreams, fantasies and fears? Little wonder that the girl had strayed from the right path. It had taken the death of several people to bring it home to him, but he was certain-sure now that the blame for all this was his as much as it was Esther's.

As the night wore away, Hammond became increasingly optimistic and almost cheerful. He was ever so when he had a job of work to do and a plan in his own head for how best to accomplish the end. In the present case, the matter was plain. He would intercept Barker and persuade him to give up Esther to him. He would then compound a felony to the extent of letting the man walk free. Marshal Hammond had bent the rules enough in the last few days that one final instance would make little difference.

Part of Hammond's optimism was derived from his working out what Barker was about and where he was heading. Fort Kerney, indeed! Why would he want to be travelling all the way up to that little place when a good deal closer lay the perfect location for a bad man to hide out in and meet up with like-minded souls? Abilene was only a few miles from here. That would be where that rascal was headed, for a bet. All that would be needful was to wait outside the town and then offer to exchange Barker's freedom for the release of Jeremiah Hammond's daughter. From Hammond's point of view, this would suit both sides. Perhaps the law in Wichita would catch up with Bob Barker at some stage or maybe they would not. What counted was having his child safe again in his home.

Esther woke to the smell of wood smoke. She sat up and Barker turned from the fire that he was lighting. 'A good morning to you. Posse or no posse on my tail, I am not setting out this day without coffee inside me. I always keep the makings in my bag. It is what you might term a peculiarity of mine.'

'I never slept out in the open before,' said Esther. 'Does one always get so cold and stiff?'

Barker laughed. 'Cold? Why, it is not even winter yet. These present conditions are nothing to speak of. Wait until you wake up with snow tickling your face as it lands on you. That's cold, let me tell you.'

'I prefer my bed, thank you. What are you going to do with me today?'

'I'm not about to do anything with you. I thought that we might ride on to the next town, where I have some friends. Once there, I will set you free and you may go your own way. If you would rather, I can leave you here when I go and you can make your own way to

Abilene on foot.'

'Abilene? Is that not one of those places full of gunfighters and suchlike?'

'Not overmuch, no. It is a cow town. Like Wichita, only a sight rougher. The law there is not too well organized, which is why it suits me and others of the same brand to stay there when we do not feel up to meeting folk like your pa.'

They each had two cups of strong black coffee and some bread. Then Barker tidied up the shelter and helped Esther onto the horse. The most that could be expected was that that they could proceed at a walk, with a little trotting thrown in when the beast felt up to it, burdened as it was with two riders.

When once they were on their way, Barker said, 'I have been thinking on what you told me last night. You took a wrong turning because your father was strict on sinning and looseness and with me it was altogether the other thing.'

'How do you mean? What other thing?'

'My own father is dead now and I do not wish to speak ill of him. Howsoever, he was an old sinner and we learned nothing from him as children about the right way to live.'

'Didn't he take you to church or teach you about stuff?'

'Not he,' said Barker, with a brief laugh. 'He did not much care what mischief we got up to, as long as we were not caught. If a neighbour came telling tales of us, he would whip us and ask how we dared to make him at outs with those in the nearby area. The lesson that I learned from all that was that the biggest sin of all was getting caught.'

'Why,' said Esther, 'that is just the same as me. As long as nobody found out what I was up to, I figured that everything was fine.'

'See now, that is what you might call a curious circumstance. You was raised strictly and learned to hide your misdeeds and I was not raised at all in that line, but still picked up the same lesson.'

'You think we are alike?'

'Lord forbid,' said Barker, sincerely. 'I was thinking more that you have to teach little ones about right and wrong in a way that they know those things in their hearts. It is too late for me, but not for you. I hate to think of your following a similar road to my own.'

'It is not what I aim for,' said the girl.

10

Marshal Hammond reached Abilene at about 8 a.m. Even at this early hour, the place was a hive of industry, with the cattle yards full and more steers arriving by the minute. Although not a large town, Abilene was a well-known one. In 1870, Thomas Smith, better known as 'Bear River' Smith, was the marshal of Abilene. He went out to a nearby farm and attempted to serve a warrant on Moses Miles. In the course of the gun battle which developed from this simple operation, Smith was wounded. As he lay there, utterly helpless, Miles clubbed him insensible with the butt of his rifle and then cut off the marshal's head with an axe. The following year, 'Wild' Bill Hickok was appointed marshal. This ended with his being sacked after accidentally shooting dead one of his deputies.

Abilene was not the lively place that it had been a few years ago, but it was still the kind of town which tolerated lawlessness more than most. Hammond had no doubt at all that Bob Barker would come riding down the road into Abilene and, with a little good fortune, they would be able to conduct their business pleasantly and then never set eyes upon each other again. The only possible fly in the ointment was that Barker's grudge against Marshal Hammond for his role in wiping out the man's family might be too great for him to receive amicably the offer of amnesty in exchange for the freeing of Esther. In that case, it might come to blows or even worse.

* * *

Esther said, 'I'm sorry that it was my father as killed yours. How did it happen?'

'It was a stupid business. He went out to my pa's farm with a couple of deputies from Wichita. It was nothing to do with him, I do not even know why he was there. There was shooting and when it was over both my father and two of my brothers were killed dead.'

'Still, you can't be sure that it was my father that killed them. It could have been the deputies.'

'That is true. But he surely killed a good friend of mine a while back near Linton. It is right and proper for you to stick up for your pa, but he and I are not likely to become friends.'

It was a beautiful, autumn day — a day to be glad about the world and all that was in it. Esther hoped that she and her father might still have a future together. The expedition to Wichita with Chris had been fun in a way, but she would not like to think of living so on a permanent basis. The lifestyle that this man behind her lived — never knowing from one day to the next if he would be arrested or killed — must be a truly terrible one.

* * *

If his calculations were correct, then Barker would not get to Abilene for at least an hour yet. Which meant, thought Hammond, that he would have time for some breakfast before meeting his adversary. He found a cheap eating house and ordered some bacon and eggs. This he washed down with copious quantities of strong coffee, until he felt a little better. It was not the first time, not by a long sight, that he had rode all through the night and then conducted some business of this nature at the end of it, but in recent years, he had noticed that such games were taking more of a toll upon him.

Most of those sitting at nearby tables were carrying firearms and so Hammond did not think that anybody would object to his preparing for action here. He took from his bag a small copper flask of powder and a box of percussion caps. He did not look for there to be any gunplay this morning, but doubtless the possibility existed and so he meant to be ready.

First, he emptied the charges from all five chambers of the Dragoon. He always did this if he wanted to be perfectly sure of his gun. Sometimes, powder left in a chamber for too long has a habit of becoming damp and failing to take fire. This can be fatal if you are depending upon your shot to kill an adversary.

He had to winkle the balls out with a toothpick, but eventually the cylinder was completely empty. He freed it from the spindle and cleaned out each chamber with a screwed up piece of paper. While Hammond was engaged in this task, the man at a nearby table said, 'Say, you don't often see cap and ball pistols like that anymore. I am surprised to see somebody in your line of work favouring such an antiquated weapon.' Hammond remembered then that he still had his star showing.

'It all depends if you wish to throw a heap of lead about or put one or two

shots just where you want them to go,'
he said.

'Mind if I join you for a moment?'
the fellow asked.

Although he was not really in the
mood for casual and inconsequential
talk, Hammond felt that it would have
been discourteous to refuse and so he
acquiesced with a shrug. The man came
over and sat down at his table.

'Don't you ever have sparks setting
off another chamber when you fire? I
have had that happen to me during the
war.'

'It need not be a problem,' said
Marshal Hammond. 'You just smear a
little fat or grease around the chamber
when once it is charged.' He showed
what he meant by wiping a little bacon
grease from his breakfast plate around
the chamber he had just filled. 'See
now, any spark will now be extin-
guished.'

The two of them chatted a little and
then Hammond excused himself and
left the eating house. He went down the

street to where he had left Buster tethered to a rail, his intention being to ride and meet Barker and his daughter.

★ ★ ★

'How long until we get to this Abilene?' asked Esther.

'Maybe an hour,' replied Bob Barker, 'Do you want to rest for a spell?'

'I would not mind walking around a bit, yes.'

So amiable and accommodating was the man she was travelling with, that Esther Hammond could hardly bring herself to believe that he really was a villain. He was solicitous of her welfare, treated her with enormous respect and had urged her to repent and follow the right road; although of course he had not put the case in those exact words. She had known men from her father's church who she would not have cared to be alone with under these circumstances. Strange to relate, the fellow was an absolute gentleman.

'What will you do when once you have unburdened yourself of me in Abilene?' the girl asked.

'I have one or two irons in various fires,' replied Barker. 'I'm sure that I shall pick up with one or two friends and we will undertake some enterprise or other.'

'Is that the roundabout way of saying that you will rob a bank or something?' said Esther.

'You got that right,' said Barker. 'Come, are you stretched enough now?' They got back on the horse and carried on towards Abilene.

★　★　★

Now it often happens that the bitterest tragedies are precipitated by the most trifling and inconsequential causes. Death and disaster can be triggered by some random misunderstanding, even one as simple as mistaking one man for another as he walks down the street. This is just what happened in the case of Jeremiah Hammond.

The night before Marshal Hammond arrived in Abilene, a set of drunken cowboys were celebrating reaching the end of the Chisholm Trail after a long and arduous cattle drive from Texas. Seven of them had started out drinking, but one had become separated from his friends and ended up disputing in a bar-room. The result was that he had been picked up by the town marshal and locked up overnight.

The remaining six boys from the original party had not received word of their comrade's misfortune until after dawn that morning. They had been moving round a fair bit throughout the night, from location to location and had more or less forgotten about their friend. Now though, they were filled with wrath and determined to have the matter out with the marshal who had had the gall to tackle one of their band in this high-handed fashion. That they had all six of them been drinking the whole night long, did not help matters nor make it any likelier that they would reach a peaceful and satisfactory conclusion.

It was at the moment that the six cowboys were marching towards the marshal's office to see about having their fellow worker freed, that the marshal himself came striding straight towards them, with a look upon his face that suggested that he was in no mood for any foolishness and would brook no debate. It was of course not the Abilene town marshal, but rather Jeremiah Hammond. He had a star on his jacket and looked set for business and so it was an easy mistake for them to make. The six men spread out across his way and stood firm, indicating that they were looking for a confrontation.

'Well boys,' said Hammond, in a brisk but not unfriendly way, 'what will you have? I am in somewhat of a hurry, so state your business quickly.'

'We are looking for Ben Saddler, you whore's son and you had best tell us right now where you have him kept!' was the reply.

Much as he was in a hurry, Marshal Hammond did not take at all to being spoken to in this wise. 'You had better watch that mouth of yours, mister. Talk like that will land you in trouble before you are very much older. Have you not heard that, 'A soft answer turneth away wrath, but strong words provoketh a rebuke'? That's the Bible text and I can tell you now that you carry on so and I am just the man to rebuke you. All of you now, step aside. I have matters to attend to.'

This forthright and uncompromising attitude did not recommend itself to the men blocking Hammond's path. One of them spat on the sidewalk and said, 'You better change your tune. Otherwise, you will have trouble on your hands.'

Despite his pressing engagement, Marshal Hammond did not propose to allow this sort of thing. He flipped his jacket to one side, exposing the pistol that was tucked into his belt. He said, 'That is enough talk, now. Clear the road, so that I may pass. If you do not, then the consequences will be upon your own heads.' He had not failed to notice that all six of the young men blocking his way were carrying weapons, but did not believe that they would really be prepared to risk death over what was evidently a simple case of mistaken identity.

* * *

As Bob Barker came into Abilene, he said to his young passenger, 'Well young lady, here is where you and me part company. It has been nice visiting with you, even if the circumstances of our meeting were not what one might call promising.'

'Oh, as to that, I think that things might have worked out well enough. I have had a lively time this last week, but I would not care to live so as a regular routine.'

'I will take you into the centre of town,' said Barker. 'There you can find the telegraph office and other useful places. You have money?'

'Yes, yes I do. Thank you.'

'Now recollect what I said to you, as touching upon your father. I was hot for killing him not twenty four hours since, but for your sake and not his, I will forego that vengeance. You go right back to him and tell him you are sorry for what you done and that you will study to be a better person in the future. Will you do that?'

'Yes, I will.'

'Do you promise me?'

'Yes, I promise.'

'Well, that's a mercy. My sort of life is not one for a good girl such as yourself. I can't think what you were about. Set mind to what your pa tells you and go back to Linton with him.'

As they came to Main Street, a surprising and unlooked for sight met their eyes. They were approaching a bunch of men from the rear. These fellows gave every impression of being about to launch an attack and the object of their assault was a man dressed soberly in black, with a shiny silver star gleaming upon his jacket. It was plain that they had arrived just as this affair was about to reach a climax.

'Oh, please help my father!' said Esther urgently.

'Help your father? That is not likely.'

'He cannot stand against all those men.'

'He did well enough yesterday,' muttered Barker, 'All right, get down now.' He helped lower her to the ground and then dismounted himself. He said to the frightened girl, 'Run along out of harm's way now. I will do what I may.'

Bob Barker walked up to within twenty feet of the group of men who appeared to be menacing the marshal and said loudly, 'Now what's to do here?'

The cowboys whirled round to face this unexpected interruption. One of them said, 'What's it to you? Are you the law as well?'

Barker laughed out loud at this question. He shook his head and said, 'Nothing of the sort. But you might say that I have an interest in this fellow's welfare. It don't signify how. Just you men go on about your affairs now and we will not fall out.'

For a second or so, everything balanced upon the edge of a knife. All the cowboys really wanted was to find their missing friend and be reunited with him. They had not taken much to the way in which the marshal had spoken to them, but would probably have overlooked this. Now though, they were being squeezed from two different directions. That this squeezing was being done by only two men, when there were six of them, all carrying, sat ill with two of the more hot-blooded types in the group. One of these men said, 'If you know what is good for you, you will walk on now on the other side of the road and leave this alone.'

'Can't be done, my friend,' said Bob Barker cheerfully. 'Made a promise to a young lady and I always keep such promises. That man yonder is no particular friend of mine, but on this occasion, he and I stand together. Take him on and I come too.'

'Do you say so?' said one of the cowboys, who then drew his pistol and commenced firing at Barker.

11

Although there were six armed men on one side and only two on the other, these bare odds were misleading in the extreme. Both Jeremiah Hammond and Bob Barker had spent their entire lives using firearms and were perfectly familiar not only with the practicalities of shooting, but also with maintaining their heads under fire. It is one thing to fool around from time to time, as all the cowboys had, with shooting at bottles balanced on fenceposts; it is quite another thing to take careful aim when somebody is trying to blow your head off.

The instant that Barker saw the boy reaching for his gun, he had dropped to the sidewalk and rolled down into the road. The young fellow who was shooting at him was, as has been mentioned, tolerably good at shooting fixed and inanimate objects like bottles and rocks, but was less able to hit a moving target. He fired five shots, none of which came within two feet of Barker.

As Barker threw himself down, Jeremiah Hammond moved into action. He was a little vexed with the outlaw for turning up in this way and having the temerity to represent himself as being about to rescue a marshal from this bunch of roughnecks. Nevertheless, it provided the opportunity that Hammond needed to draw his piece. He did so, cocking it at the same time. The six men all had their backs to him now and he could not bring himself to shoot anyone in the back. When the first shots were being fired though, he marked the man who was doing the shooting and reckoned that this man at least was fair game and could be justifiably shot. The marshal fired twice at him, hitting him firstly in his trunk and then following that up with a shot to his head.

The other five cowboys were taken

aback by finding themselves in the midst of a gun battle. All they had really been after was throwing their weight about a little and showing off. As things had now reached this pitch though, they all of them felt honour bound to draw their weapons and start shooting.

Barker, who had not yet fired, now drew his own pistol and rose to his feet. He singled out the weakest-willed of the young men, a boy of nineteen who had pulled his gun out and now stood there looking bewildered, with no idea of what to do next. It was an easy target and Barker shot him twice. Meanwhile, the marshal had ducked into a store and now leaned out to fire at the four remaining men.

Barker ran down the street a way, giving at first sight the look of a man fleeing from the fight. In truth though, he was preventing any of the other combatants from drawing down on him, getting a good aim and also encouraging them to waste their ammunition. He stopped running and without any warning dropped once more to the ground and fired at another man. This time, he missed.

The cowboys had recovered from their shock at finding themselves embroiled in a gunfight of this nature and were crouching behind water butts, boxes and other such things which were piled outside the stores which lined this part of Main Street. One of the men was foolish enough to stand up so that he could get a clear shot at Barker, whereupon he was instantly cut down by a bullet from Marshal Hammond. He and Barker, both experienced gunfighters, almost seemed to be working in tandem. The problem comes in such cases from the rank amateur who has no idea how to conduct himself and therefore behaves in an alarmingly unexpected way that can take the professionals aback. A man of this sort can disrupt things badly, as Hammond found to his cost. He had fired four times, killing two men, which was not bad going, all things considered. Keenly aware that he only had one bullet remaining and realising that he might have done worse than hang on to that other pistol which the deputies in Wichita had loaned him, Hammond stopped for a moment to wonder how he would be able to carry on after firing his pistol one more time.

Few activities are more hazardous during a shootout than stopping to think about your next move. For it was just as Jeremiah Hammond's attention wandered from the here and now that one young man jumped to his feet and ran straight at the marshal, where he was mostly concealed behind the doorway of the hardware store. Nobody with any prior knowledge of how to survive in a battle of this kind would have dreamed for a moment of making such a rash charge: running straight towards somebody firing from a protected position. Hammond's mind was elsewhere to the extent that he failed to react to the threat until the young fellow was six feet from him. Then they both fired simultaneously.

The marshal felt a searing, burning pain in his shoulder and knew at once that he had been hit. It was small comfort for him to see the man who had shot him fall lifeless to the sidewalk, with Hammond's last bullet lodged in his brain.

Bob Barker was feeling that special exhilaration that comes from surviving a hail of gunfire. He had not looked for such an enterprise this morning, but now that it had come, he was pretty well content at the way that it was all turning out. Between the two of them, he and the marshal were bidding fair to settle every one of those cowboys. It was then that Barker saw a sight which chilled his blood. Esther Hammond, far from going to seek shelter, was now running towards the scene of battle because she had just seen her father get shot.

'Go back!' shouted Barker, but the girl did not hear him. She had seen her father go down and nothing was more important to her in this world or the next than speaking to him for what might be one last time and begging his forgiveness. She did not know it but the case was not as desperate as she thought. Hammond had certainly gone down after being shot, but he was not out of the game yet. Although he was bleeding pretty freely from a flesh wound in his shoulder, he still had the presence of mind to snatch up the gun of the man who had shot him. Then, he too saw Esther dashing towards him across the street. He too shouted, 'No, get back!' but his daughter took no more notice of this than she had of Barker's similar exhortation.

Marshal Hammond forced himself to his feet and even managed a few faltering steps. If the two cowboys had been looking in his direction, it would have been all up with him, because it was all he could do to remain upright, let alone raise his arm and fire a pistol. Fortunately, they were both staring at the spectacle of Bob Barker, who had jumped up and was shouting, 'Cease firing, this girl has no part of this. Hold your fire.'

One of the cowboys stayed crouched down where he was, whether he was heeding Barker's cries or had just had enough of the fight was open to question. His companion though, seeing that one of his opponents had let down his guard, stood up and deliberately shot Bob Barker twice. The first bullet shattered his wrist, but the second took him through the chest. There was little opportunity for him to rejoice at this victory though, because Jeremiah Hammond had summoned up his last reserves of strength and raised the pistol in his hand, shooting the cowboy through the back of the head. The lone survivor of what might not inaptly be termed a massacre, sprang to his feet at this point and sprinted off down the street.

Slowly and unsteadily, Hammond stepped off the sidewalk and towards the spot where his daughter was holding the hand of the dying man. When he reached them, the marshal sank to his knees and said to Barker, 'Well, we took them all right.'

Barker tried to smile, but grimaced instead. 'I am shot to bits, Hammond.'

'I mind you would not have been so but for trying to save my daughter. I know it and cannot give you thanks enough.'

Barker made a dismissive gesture with his head, as if to say that this was not worth mentioning. Then he spoke one last time. He spoke to Esther, saying, 'Recollect what I told you on the road, you hear me?' Then he closed his eyes and did not reopen them.

Now that the shooting had stopped, people began coming out of the stores and extricating themselves from the various undignified places that they had been hiding from the gunfire. The five corpses lying scattered in front of the hardware store excited interest, but nobody wanted to involve themselves in the scene taking place in the road, where a badly wounded man was embracing a young woman over the lifeless body of another victim of the fighting.

Both Jeremiah Hammond and his daughter were prey to strong emotions at the end of what was to become a legendary event in the history of Abilene. For his part, Hammond saw somebody kneeling besides him who was no longer a fractious and disobedient child, but rather a person who was, to all intents and purposes, a grown woman. Esther found herself looking not at a stern and unforgiving parent, but a tired, middle-aged man who was looking worn out and borne down by cares. These new perspectives came as something of a shock to them both.

* * *

The journey back to Linton was not an easy one. Once his shoulder was patched up, Hammond needed to rest for a few days. He and Esther booked into Abilene's only respectable hotel for this period. The town marshal was not pleased at the course of events and could not for the life of him make out how a lawman could have ended up fighting side by side with a known criminal such as Bob Barker. It was a mystery that neither Jeremiah Hammond nor his daughter were inclined to clear up for him.

While they were staying at the hotel, Hammond gave his daughter to understand that he was informed as to every aspect of her life since leaving Linton. He offered no condemnation, but rather bent his efforts to destroying every scrap of evidence that remained. This included burning the $100 bills which she still had in her possession.

'I do not propose,' said Marshal Hammond to his daughter, 'ever to mention or discuss this affair again, when we are back in Linton. You will find that there is a certain amount of suspicion attached to you, but the night watchman who your friend assaulted has now dug up and left. This means that there is no case to answer, as he was the only witness. Still and all, word has spread about what took place and you will find folks look sideways at you. It can't be helped.'

'I'm sorry,' began the girl, but Hammond cut in, not brutally but in a reasonable and matter-of-fact way.

'That's nothing to the purpose, Esther. I am not asking to hear confessions of remorse. I have been to blame in the past perhaps for caring about such outward acts of piety. If you are sorry, then show it to others.'

'What about that fellow in Wichita?' asked Esther, 'You know of that?'

'The same thing,' said the marshal. 'I will say nothing of the matter and if you are sorry then try to live better from now on. You are my daughter and I love you.'

This was the first time in her entire life that she had heard her father use the word 'love' in connection with her and Esther found her eyes filling with tears. They embraced.

*　　*　　*

It would be pleasant to relate that Jeremiah Hammond and his daughter never fell out again and that the episode at Wichita marked a complete change in how the two of them were with each other. Life is not really like that and there were to be many occasions in the future when Marshal Hammond wanted to reproach his daughter with her infamous conduct. He somehow managed to hold his tongue though and keep his own counsel.

One unexpected beneficiary of this new way of life was Caroline Hammond, who found her star rising to no small degree in the household — being consulted now about many aspects of her niece's life, from the clothes she wore to the dances that she might attend. Nearly losing his only child had

had the profoundest effect upon Marshal Hammond and it was widely noticed that he was a changed man on his return from Wichita and Abilene.

The very first night that he brought Esther back to her home, Jeremiah Hammond sat up late, reading his Bible. He prayed chiefly for himself, asking the Lord to soften his heart and help him to be a better and more understanding parent. Before he slept, he read once more that text which suggests that the sins of the fathers are visited upon the children. He closed the Good Book and muttered to himself, 'Not always. Not here, if I know anything about it.' Then he turned out the lamp and went to sleep.

THE END

We do hope that you have enjoyed reading this large print book.

Did you know that all of our titles are available for purchase?

We publish a wide range of high quality large print books including:
Romances, Mysteries, Classics
General Fiction
Non Fiction and Westerns

Special interest titles available in large print are:
The Little Oxford Dictionary
Music Book, Song Book
Hymn Book, Service Book

Also available from us courtesy of Oxford University Press:
Young Readers' Dictionary
(large print edition)
Young Readers' Thesaurus
(large print edition)

For further information or a free brochure, please contact us at:
Ulverscroft Large Print Books Ltd.,
The Green, Bradgate Road, Anstey,
Leicester, LE7 7FU, England.
Tel: (00 44) 0116 236 4325
Fax: (00 44) 0116 234 0205

Other titles in the
Linford Western Library:

DUEL OF THE OUTLAWS

John Russell Fearn

The inhabitants of Twin Pines, Arizona lead uneventful, happy lives — until the sudden arrival of Black Yankee and his gang. They shoot the sheriff, take over the place, and Twin Pines spirals downwards into an outlaw town, with lawlessness and sudden death the norm. When Thorn Tanworth, son of the sheriff, returns from his travels, to everyone's astonishment he establishes a mutually beneficial partnership with Black Yankee. But then the two men begin fighting each other for control of the town . . .

KID FURY

Michael D. George

The remote settlement of War Smoke lies quiet — until the calm is shattered by a gunshot. Marshal Matt Fallen and his deputy Elmer spring into action to investigate. Then another shot rings out, and cowboy Billy Jackson's horse gallops into town, dragging its owner's corpse in the dust: one boot still caught in its stirrup, and one hand gripping a smoking gun. Meanwhile, the paths of hired killer Waco Walt Dando and gunfighter Kid Fury are set to converge on War Smoke . . .